SILVER MOON

GREAT NOVELS
OF
EROTIC DOMINATION
AND SUBMISSION

NEW TITLES EVERY MONTH

www.smbooks.co.uk

TO FIND OUT MORE ABOUT OUR READERS' CLUB
WRITE TO;

SILVER MOON READER SERVICES;
Suite 7,
Mayden House,
Long Bennington Business Park,
Newark NG23 5DJ
Tel; 01400283488

YOU WILL RECEIVE A FREE MAGAZINE OF EXTRACTS
FROM OUR EXTENSIVE RANGE OF EROTIC FICTION
ABSOLUTELY FREE. YOU WILL ALSO HAVE THE CHANCE
TO PURCHASE BOOKS WHICH ARE EXCLUSIVE TO OUR
READERS' CLUB

***

NEW AUTHORS ARE WELCOME

Please send submissions to;
The Editor; Silver Moon books
Suite 7Long Bennington Business Park
Newark NG23 5DJ

All characters and events depicted are entirely fictitious; any resemblance to anyone living or dead is entirely coincidental

WHEN THE MASTER SPEAKS

by

Josephine Scott

CHAPTER 1
JULY 1869.

My Dear Sister,
    Sister, I have felt rage from Papa before, when I broke the fine china dish that was his mother's wedding present to him, when I did stand knee deep in the river and search for fish, my skirts held up in a shameful and wanton fashion (so Papa said) and I felt then the terrible force of his rage and the terrible sting of the strap.

... but stay, let me not think of the strap for a brief moment, though the whistle of its falling echoes loud within my head. Perhaps that is why I write this letter to you, to purge such thoughts and also in the hope, nay the prayer, that one way I will be free to send it to you! and you will know what became of your sister Clarisse after I ran away -

Let me speak first of London town where it is fine and warm. Let me tell you here in London there are people - so many people! You would not begin to believe how many people could live in one city, for sure it makes our local towns look so provincial. And people smile when they hear my voice for I speak with the voice of a country girl and I hate it.

Ah Sister, I can see you disapprove of me even as I write these lines! You always said we should be proud of what we are, country people, the salt of the earth. But who knows, it may be you will never see these words. They are to ease my mind as much as they are to be read by you one fine day.

I do wonder how are you all there, and how little Marcia is, has she recovered from her cough? Here they say there is a fine cure to be found in honey and mullein, but of course Mama will have her own ideas of what she should give such a small and frail child. How is Thomas, I wonder, does he miss his big Sister taking care of him, and the pony? And is Papa raging with indignation at my departure? How will I ever go back?

I will never go back!

Sophie, I can delay no more, I must tell you what happened before I left.

Papa told me to clean the brass in the church. I went with a bad heart for I do so hate the brass in our church for all that it is fine and been brought from bequests by our local landowners in honour and remembrance of the dear departed. It is too carved and intricate, Sophie, as you will now find, as Papa is bound to ask you to do it. Nay, order you to do it. It has many corners and curves, and Papa does so like to have every corner gleaming! So I was in church with a bad heart, polishing away wishing with all my mind that our benefactors had left the money to the church so we could have new curtains and altar cloths and not brass, when Peter James came in from the farm.

You know only too well, dear sister, that Peter James is not a religious man, he had not called into the church for a prayer or meditation on the Scriptures for the day. Nor did he come to pray for the relief from the foot and mouth raging through his Master's herd.

He came because he saw me enter the church and not quite close the door after me.

I did not wish to close the door. I wished for some of the summer heat and warmth to penetrate the cold dark prayer heavy stones, that the kiss of Nature would come into the works of Man for our church is so dark and so dour I feel my very spirits depressed at setting foot across the doorstep.

I did not wish to close the door for I saw Peter James in the distance and I wondered if he would see me. I did make it clear when at market that I was interested, did I not toss my dark curls and flash my dark eyes and smiled at him with lips which I had bitten into redness and flaunted the breasts God gave me to interest a man? And did I not see the answering smile and look he gave me, for I have long since learned to read a man, as you will one day, dear Sophie, my quiet subdued sister!

For I did sore long for a man's arms round me.

Oh sister, it is a sin, I know it is! but I did so long for a man to have an arm around me and press his lips to mine and open up the fire that is burning deep within me! And these were the thoughts I took - greviously sinful that they were - into the church.

And as I stood with rag and vinegar and salt for polish and the candlestick in my hand, so did Peter James enter the church and without a word take the rag and candlestick from my hands, and draw me to his breast. And I felt the work hard muscles and the softness of sun kissed skin for he do work outside and is a fine upstanding man for sure. And sister, he kissed me with summer in his mouth and fire in his loins and I did cry out with the pleasure of it.

Down on the carpet before the altar did we go, forgetting where we were, forgetting what we had been taught for in our minds I am sure was nothing more than the feelings which raged through us, for I felt his manhood stiffen against me and I felt my own answering body yield to his - and we were in that position, he about to do that unthinkable act, when Papa came in.

Well! I have seen Papa in many a rage, but sister, I have never felt anything like this! Peter James hustled out, fled the church even as Papa roared after him that his Master would be told and retribution rained down on him. And I stood, skirts awry and blouse awry for he had sought and I gave a breast into his warm sunny hand. I must have been a sight, stood with hair atumble and my eyes aflame with the feelings I had. I know my bosom heaved with breaths so deep it was as if I would take into myself the whole atmosphere of the church and breathe it out suffused with life!

And Papa looked at me and I saw in his eyes the truth. He lusted after me.

He seethed in his anger and rage at his own feelings and what I was about to do before the high altar, and he the Vicar of this church too! I knew my time had come. That this would be a punishment not to equal any other I had ever had.

I know not what was in his mind. He left the church locking it behind him, without so much as a single word passing between us.

And I sat down on the step where so soon before I had lain in willing surrender to Peter James' arms, and I cried. Cried for hunger and for fear of what was to happen to me.

And, as I wish to be honest in this account to you, dear sister, I confess too I cried that I still retained my maidenhead, for I would sore like to have given it up!

Sister, I stayed locked in the church. The sun rose high in the sky and burned through the windows onto the gravestones over which we walk without thought every Sunday, and I fancied the sun would warm the corpses amouldering there and raise their spirits up so they would want to stand up and stretch their limbs into the warmth and lifegiving rays. And I sat afeared that the stones would rise up.

Then I was overcome with a desire to piss so hard that it was a pain. I fought the pain but it overcame me and I knew I could not wait, so I crept into the vestry and there relieved myself in a corner. Papa will find that smell later and know what took place there, but what was I to do, sister? What would you have done?

And then the sun left the sky, climbed down to go away and leave the world to the darkness. An owl hooted outside and bats swooped around the windows casting tiny flickering shadows.

And I was more afeared than I had been before.

For if the spirits are to walk then it is in the night they walk and I knew they would not like my being there. And I sat alone, huddled at the foot of the altar where the Cross of Our Lord Jesus Christ might protect me. Oh the dreams I had and the fears I had and the monsters I conjured!

I prayed many a prayer that night, sister, but confess to you I did not ask forgiveness, for Almighty God would smile on love in the sun. I felt I did no bad thing, no matter what Papa might have thought. For were not virgins sacrificed for crops in the past?

I heard your voice in the morning, oh so early, calling through the lock to me - how sweet a voice, how kind you were, how good to hear a living sound that did not mean ghosts or ghoulies! Never have I loved a person so much as I loved you that moment, my sister! But without the key there was nothing you could do for me.

Then you went away as I knew you would.

And Papa came.

He came with Verger Pearson, a hard man with no mercy in his eyes, and he smiled a cold hard smile that was worse than the sharpest slap across the face I have ever had. There was Peter James' master, Farmer Gray, the Blacksmith, Adam Smith, with Joseph Olberon from the Plough Inn, and with cold Mister Tilling from the village.

The church elders gathered in one place. Papa locked the door behind them and they stood, cold and hard and yet smiling. How the elders do love a punishment, most especially when it be a fresh young woman to receive the strap!

"Daughter, you have sinned against God and man in this holy place."

And I stood up and faced them, Papa, Verger and all. I smiled at them.

I said "I have not sinned, I did that which comes naturally to those who are young and comely."

And they started back as if I had struck them one by one yet altogether.

"Your sin is compounded from your own mouth, young lady." And Joseph Olberon produced ropes from a pocket. Farmer Gray took a bench from the back of the church and stood it in the centre and Papa took my arm and dragged me to the bench and pushed me down so I laid along it. Mr Olberon took my wrists and ankles and tied them to the legs of the bench so there was no way I could escape. My face was pressed against the cold scratchy wood and I was much afeared then, sister, I can assure you! I was more afeared than I had been alone when the ghosts walked in the church, creaked the pews and touched my curls and when Satan prowled around the outside of my thought!

"What think you, gentlemen?" Papa sounded so satisfied, and they had not even begun!

"I think we should beat the Devil out of her." That was Mister Tilling.

And even as I lay uncomfortable flat on the bench, my face pressed down, my body waiting for what would surely come I felt a move to laugh aloud, for surely they knew afore they came that they would beat me! It is the punishment the elders give for all disobedience, and I remembered in that moment that Peter James had been flogged on this very bench, birched fifty times they said, for consorting with the farmer's daughter. It seemed the birching did no good, for there he had been about to consort with me.

And I knew too that it was said to put fear in my mind and trembling into my body. And it did.

"You be the oldest here, sir, and the most Elder of our church, may I suggest you start?" Papa, how kind you were to delay your own pleasure for so long! My skirts were ripped away by a firm hand I could not begin to see. My pantaloons were down and I laid, bare and waiting and much ashamed, before the gathered eyes of the elders of our church. I am sure my cheeks were much flushed, for sure my face was!

Old Mister Tilling may be an old man, sister of mine, but be sure he has a firm arm, especially when that arm ends with a strap well worn by Papa on our backsides over the years! Ten times old Mister Tilling lashed me with that strap and ten times I cried out.

But oh that was nothing to Mister Olberon who is much strengthened with the lifting of barrels of ale and pulling of the pints in the Plough every night! Twice as hard and half across my thighs did Mister Olberon strap me and I knew for sure I would not easily forget this!

And Adam Smith, hands well strengthened with all the work of the forge, strapped me even harder, were that possible! but of course I grew sorer as each blow landed and went across those already there. For all that I was already hurting and afire with the awful strap I knew he was stronger even than Mister Olberon.

Awash with tears, sister, I awaited the Farmer for he too had a strong arm, and I was not mistaken, how I screamed as the strap hit me another ten times.

And Verger Pearson, he looks like a weak man, perhaps that was why he came near to last when I was red sore and weeping heartily and crying out for mercy even though I knew there was none there, these men were the elders and I had offended against their church. And Verger Pearson laid on his ten with a firm hand that near broke me.

And then it was Papa's turn and he put into it all he had in him, all his anger and his lust for he knew I had seen that lust when he saw my bosom exposed and my skirts awry and I know he wanted me for himself and it is the biggest sin of all to want your own daughter. In his anger he lashed me so hard I thought the strap would break on me!

"Gentlemen, have the sins been beaten out of my daughter?" and it was said in such a way I knew full well they had, all of them, every last man of them, enjoyed my suffering and the taking part in inflicting it on me. And I knew full well that given a chance they would do it over again, another ten times each and delight in the strap hitting flesh now surely scored with blood!

"I would say the Devil has gone out of her." Mister Tilling again, pronouncing judgement, with a tone of regret I could clear enough hear. How I hated them, every last one, for the pain I felt and the tears I shed and the shame of it all! And even as I thought all this, I wondered what they would do this time to Peter James, and I feared for his skin for surely he would be publicly whipped at the post!

Then I had to lie there and listen to a sermon on sin and morality and foul violation of the sacred holiness of the church and all the time I felt nothing but the terrible pain which swept across my backside and my thighs, and the tears which choked me and the hunger which stalked me even at that time.

Then Papa forbade me to tell you or any of the others or indeed dear Mama what I had had to endure. And I was to have nothing but bread and water for a month and be confined to my room when I was not cleaning every inch of the church, the floor to be scrubbed, the walls to be washed the pews to be polished to cleanse it all of my sin.

Sister, I could not stand the thought of that! A thrashing, yes, well, for all that it was so hard, sixty strokes! Would ever you believe anyone could take sixty strokes? Well, I did, and I suffered for my sin of wanting Peter James. But I would not wash the church! But then I said nothing but stood up so carefully when the ropes were untied and curtsied to each of the elders and begged pardon when bidden. And the eyes gleamed in the darkness of the church and the lust came at me in waves and any one of them would have borne me down to that carpet before the high altar and taken my maidenhead.

But I wanted nothing to do with old men who smelled of stale ale and smoke, of old age and piety, when underneath they sinned every bit as much as I did! For sure every one of them should have knelt in that church for a day and a half and asked for absolution from their sin of lust and desire!

So Sophie dear, I crept away with a bundle of clothes and my prayer book for companion and I asked the carter to take me to the railway station for all that it was hard to sit on the plank without covering with the bruises telling me I had been thrashed. And as he knew me well, he said he would, and ask Papa for the money when he got back.

How small a revenge that is! But how much pleasure it gave me!

And I approached the first gentleman I saw, for fear and loneliness and sheer desperation makes bold women of us all, to ask if he would pay for me to go to London if I sat with him during the journey and entertained him.

And Sophie he smiled at me and said he would be delighted. And this man, his name is Albert Lymardson, was going to London where he lives, and he took me with him and here I am, installed in his house right in the very heart of London, and I am his maid and servant, and it is a pleasure to work for him.

But I am not sure I am going to stay. For he is old and I need a young man to love me. I am awakened by the thought of Peter James' sunlit hands and body and Sophie, I need a young man!

My thoughts are with you often, and dear Mama, and the baby and everyone. I wish I could send this to you but Papa would see it and confiscate it and he might even find me! And that dear sister, would never do. But one day I will find a way to get this to you so you know your loving sister is alive and well.

And sister, I pray you never have to suffer at the hands of the elders as I did, for the bruises took a month to go, a month of sitting slow and careful and Albert Lymardson never to know what happened to me.

Because - a small confession comes here that is for my eyes alone, on a page I will never send - I dream of that thrashing and I am aflame with desire.

God help me!

CHAPTER 2
JULY 1969

July pressed hard against the huge windows of the High Court. Barristers rushed around in torn gowns and horsehair wigs, trailing impatience and legal knowledge with the assurance only such a high standing could give them. Secretaries clicked here and there on spiked heels and skirts that wouldn't have looked out of place in a strip show. At least Lauren thought they were secretaries. They wore no badge, yet managed to look important.

Court officials frowned their superior frowns and hustled people to and fro, escorting them to an invisible chalk mark outside Courtroom doors.

A window was tilted open here and there, showing a glimpse of burning blue sky and letting in hot almost turgid air.

Lauren looked up and found a man opposite staring at her, dark inscrutable eyes piercing through to her soul. His Van Dyke beard perfectly suited the small face, the neatly combed hair, the gloved hands (gloves? in July?) atop a walking stick crowned with silver. Narrow wrists. Thin wrists. Steel strong. Holding a cane, a riding crop, a whip?

The entire thought took less than a second. In that time she had taken in his appearance, registered a certain dominant attitude about his rigid body and inflexible look, imagined steel hard wrists wielding something thin and sharp with devastating strength and felt herself plunging towards orgasm.

He came over, smiled at her, tapped her lightly with the end of the walking stick.

"I have that effect on some women," and he was gone, striding away, a calm enigmatic smile touching his lips, now he had merged into the busy scene, merged and vanished from her life. Lauren almost collapsed, trying to regain some self control, trying to pull her thoughts back together again. How had he done that? With telepathy? Whatever it was, he had done it and it was -

Frustrating and yet satisfying at the same time.

Quite shattering!

She was shattered, shivering. She would not go back to her regular work today, she couldn't face them at the office, the dull dull workaday office, she didn't always go back after this part-time detective work. A decision taken, and whether it was imagined or real a mind meeting with a man who had brought her to orgasm with a look and a thought. Would I ever see him again? I'd have to be here again, hang around -

Lauren clutched her bag and held her breath, looking for some confidence. Perhaps she could snatch some from the clouds which hovered around these efficient and all knowing solicitors and Counsel meeting in groups. A flock of legal eagles. For a fleeting moment Lauren lost all her confidence and crowded herself against the painted wall.

Fear of rejection, of verbal abuse, of hostile looks, froze her to the small spot she occupied and it took a supreme effort of will to summon up the image she had seen in her mirror before leaving home that morning. Long wavy auburn hair, gleaming in the July sun, clear green eyes and long lashes sweeping delicate cheekbones, lips that used to smile - before she found out about rejection, verbal abuse and hostile looks from a man who said he loved her: the burden of that hideous scene of a few brief hours ago was still heavy upon her, and now that strange encounter ...

Pull yourself together, Lauren!

I'll do, she decided. Really I will. I must! The suit is smart enough to compete with the secretaries round here; the hair, well if it falls down over one eye there's little I can do about it. Courage, girl, courage. You may only be a part time Private Eye but you did your job well on this one: the divorce had been granted thanks to the evidence she had collected, but she pitied the couple she had helped to part.

Decree Nisi granted, the group hurried out.

'Bastard, that's what he was!'

Lauren tried to match a bastard to the friendly quiet spoken man she had interviewed. No, they were definitely talking about two different people. She clicked quickly away, leaving the conundrum of the man with two personalities and the raw emotion of a newly divorced wife behind her.

Lauren didn't always like her part-time job either.

She was very quiet as she left the bustle of the Strand and walked into the peace and tranquillity of Temple, worn flagstones, clicking footsteps of raven gowned jay headed Counsel hurrying here and there, pink tied papers under their arms, law books balanced as precariously as their worried frowns, clerks who ruled the lives of everyone, the men the power behind the throne, as it were.

A little later, on impulse, as she dived for her train, she took an evening paper from the news vendor at the corner of the station. She sat at the end of the row of seats, welcoming the space. Compared with the rush hour it was virtually empty. She glanced through the screaming headlines and close packed type, idly turned pages as the train rocked its way through another soot encrusted tunnel, the rushing wind echoing her rushing thoughts. The same advertisement had appeared in a box in the Situations Vacant for three days in a row. It was as if it was trying to tell her something.

A position in Fleet Street. Outside the calm of Temple, away from fountains and peaceful church, away from studious Chambers and into the bustle and dash of the newspaper world, where vans came and went, where people rushed around, and where a new job might be waiting for her.

I'll phone tomorrow.

Another decision. It seemed to take a load from her shoulders.

She left the underground train with a lighter mind. A decision taken, and whether it was imagined or real a mind meeting with a man who had brought her to orgasm with a look and a thought ...

Her car waited, a small grey 1100, in need of a wash and probably a good service too. It was time to go home.

The mobile home park was in darkness when she finally drove into the parking area, her headlights bouncing back at her from towering trees which held blackness in their branches. Light glowed in the site shop, there would be some mail, if only from her loving parents tucked away in their Spanish retreat. It would make her feel wanted.

She eased herself round the shop door, picked up her mail and smiled at Angela, the shopkeeper, deep in conversation with another resident. Safe for tonight at least. Angela did so love to talk.

Lights glowed from units, people preparing their tea, watching TV, settling down for the evening. Her own unit, her home, if she could call it that, was tucked away in a far corner, as if ashamed of itself. Dark and unwelcoming, it glowed a sullen dirty white in the limited street light provided by the park owner. Her shed, containing the toilet, hulked against the side, a small dog against a large owner, both down on their luck.

Little creatures moved in the undergrowth, rustled dark leaves, hurried about night business. Lauren shivered and quickly found her key ring.

The key grated in the lock, the light flickered before coming on, showing her the drab little place. Worn floor covering, battered units, scarred sink. God, why did I ever agree to come and live here? she cried silently, as she did every single night she opened the door.

But she knew why. Any port in a storm, when you have no home any port will do while the storm of life crashes around you. But this port was no more than a three roomed caravan, old, tired, shabbily furnished, draughty, with a loo outside covered in spiders and creepy crawlies, terrible in the middle of the night when the rain and wind made a necessary if not vital visit scary and uncomfortable. I'm going to get a chamber pot, she decided, as soon as I can!! I'll put up with that indignity to avoid the middle-of-the-night walk outside in rain and gales. But the caravan was cheap, and available. Two things that are irresistible when you need a home.

Opening the letter from her parents, she thought - I should have gone back to Spain to live with Mum and Dad. That was the millionth time at least, and for the millionth time she knew from the urging of her own body, from the violent reaction she had experienced on seeing the smooth darkly bearded man with the slim wrists, that she could never again be a simple little daughter, living without sex. How do you find sex in a community where everyone is married, where everyone knows everyone and ears are atuned for the merest hint of gossip and tattle? Find a Spaniard, perhaps, and be prepared for the comments that would bring! Catholic in everything, would they consort with an English woman?

Better to stay here, better to lick the wounds inflicted by Justin when he stormed out, after flicking her beloved records everywhere, breaking her record player, smashing the radio, and ripping up her books, because here at least she could indulge in dreams and vibrator games without bothering anyone.

As Lauren pottered, making cheese on toast, making tea without milk or sugar, she thought about her books, prompted by the lasting image of the man on the train.

American books, English books, all featuring ladies who were getting spanked, tawsed, caned and whipped, hard.

And the reason for the break-up with Justin. Not that he needed much of an excuse, it had been coming for some time. Too many late nights, unexplained phone calls, letters in plain envelopes that were swiftly hidden when she came in, it looked very much as if the relationship, conceived in a storm of passion and mutual lust, was heading for the rocks. The finding of her precious s/m books had been the final reef on which to crash.

"You're perverted!" Justin had shouted as he tore up the books, confetti of snatched body parts, words, illustrations, things she knew well, images she had creamed over in long empty nights when Justin had been flirting elsewhere. "Perverted! No woman wants to be treated like that!"

But I do! she had cried - silently - I do! I wanted you to do that to me!

Lauren switched out the overhead light, switched off the memories at the same time, sat before a tiny radio listening to bland music and bland voices, thinking.

The man on the train. Oh so sophisticated and smooth, so dark, so strong looking. So still! How still he had sat, clutching the walking stick, firm fingers slim wrists. How easy it was to transpose the walking stick into a riding crop, for surely such a man would use something sophisticated like a leather riding crop, or even - leap of thoughts, surge of feeling spreading from cheeks to pubis to thighs which quivered at the mere thought of it - even a plaited dressage whip.

The small lamp gave out a warm glow, inviting moths and daddy-long-legs into the room through the small window she had pushed open. Lauren ignored them, too busy with a fantasy to worry about creeping flying things. She'd catch them later, all of them.

Outside a car door slammed, someone shouted a greeting, someone else raised their voice and there was a crash. Then it all went silent again, only the humming and fluttering of the creatures round her lamp broke the evening silence.

Did he really speak to me? Did he really say those things, or did I imagine it?

But what should have happened, what didn't happen was -

He should have come over to me, pressed a hard edge printed card into my hand and said:

"Come."

I would have phoned the number, oh so shy, so afraid, so trembling with fear and lust because the mere thought of going to someone sends shudders, sends waves, sends creeping crawling not-to-be-denied feelings everywhere, but particularly down there. Nipples go hard -

I would phone. And he would say:

"I know who you are, I know what you want. Come. Now."

And the place would be somewhere smart and expensive, Grosvenor Square? one of the big London squares so full of elegance, money, and hidden vices. I would walk up the steps, carefully, on heels that threatened to give way under the weight of trembling knees, knickers so wet it was a wonder I could walk at all.

The door opens if by magic, but there is a man there, who gestures to me to enter, who closes the door behind me. Thick carpeted hall, rich tapestries, oil paintings of long dead people all wearing immaculate clothes and stern looks, the men with their matching Van Dyke beards, for surely he has come from another age, another time!

The smooth faced man leads me to a door, opens it after the lightest of knocks.

"There you are" and the library is there for me to see, all leather bound books with gold blocked titles, huge leather chairs, large oak desk carved richly with leaves and vines, a leather edged blotter, a gold pen stand. Here he is at home in his rightful surroundings, this man with the beard and the slim wrists who said so much with a look and a single sentence, and a way of moving that said 'I am a Master.'

The door is closed, we are alone.

"Tell me what you want" and it is an order, not a request. I must confess. I must say what is in my most secret of hearts, the place where even Justin, never Justin! could penetrate.

There, in the rich luxury of the library, with emerald green carpet and richness of leather books and chairs, the solidness of the desk, the calmness of the man with the beard and the wrists, toying so lightly with something I cannot see, a whip? a riding crop? the scent of polish and books, the scent of power and domination.

I confess:

"I want to be dominated, humiliated, subdued, thrashed. Bound if necessary, if a Master considers me worthy of being bound, so I cannot escape. Ever."

The words come spilling, they are there, trembling on the tip of the tongue, ever ready to spill, which is why Justin ultimately stormed and kicked and damaged and destroyed and walked out of my life, putting me on the street within three days, demanding his share of the flat and all that was in it and I had no comeback. I settled for a lousy smelly little home and a fantasy.

No.

Exclude Justin, exclude everything - go back. The man, his eyes and his hands and of course his wrists. Now I see what it is he holds, a riding crop. The shudder goes deep, so deep it touches my mind as well as my body.

"Come here." The words are so quietly spoken I cannot believe they are for real, that I am about to have something I have never had, but often dreamed of.

Oh so often dreamed of!

"Stand still" and I stand, hands before me, eyes down, I need no telling that is the way I must be before this man.

The crop lashes out, sharply, even through my clothes it hurts so much I cry out. I stand, burning, a single line flaring across my buttocks, my eyes and mouth open with shock.

"I hurt." And I know he means to, he is hard and cruel, this man with the beard and the wrists. "You said humiliation, and you will be humiliated. It is bad enough to bare yourself to me, but to do it in front of others" - he rings the bell sharply, a silver bell stood on the desk. The note is high and clear, it carries.

"Sir?" the smooth faced man is there again, as silent as a robot.

"Summon the staff."

"Sir." And he is gone and I feel redness creep into my face. Am I to be thrashed in front of others? Many others? Who?

They come. A cook, a maid, a gardener, the smooth faced butler. They stand, silent and aloof, disapproving looks worn as uniform. Not a word is uttered.

I follow the line of the crop, walk to the desk, lean over it as he indicates, for there is nothing to do but follow. There must have been a signal I did not see for the butler, for surely that is what he is, has appeared behind me and in front of me, my wrists are bound with leather strips, tied tight, and neatly bound round the desk drawer handle, I cannot move. My ankles are tied, tight, so tight the blood must be cut off. I cannot kick and move.

Knickers are lowered by the butler, making it worse. I feel shame, creeping shame, flush over and through me, it is coupled with the fear of what is to come, for surely everyone can already see the blazing red line writ clear across the cheeks, the line that said "I will hurt you" and it did.

And he did.

"I will not tell you what you are to have, for there can be no limit to what you should have." The crop comes down again, as hard as before, it cuts it burns I cry out I scream aloud and the people stand silent as it comes down again and again and again.

There is no end to pain. There is no depth to pain. It flares it burns it cuts to the heart it shrieks for mercy for release but none is to be found anywhere. Again again again a crop bound in leather flexible as the skin it once was finds skin that is unwilling oh so willing to take it.

God help me I take it.

God help me I have no choice with wrists and ankles bound with the desk cutting into the mound with nerves screaming for release with soft so soft breasts crushed against the top and my breath marking the smooth polish she would have to polish it again tomorrow the maid with the short skirt and bland disapproving face watching me being thrashed oh if only they weren't there so often I think of them being there eyes on my body calculating scheming wondering if I should make that much noise would they make that much noise do they make that much noise does he beat them too - as the crop lands over and over and over -

"You can go" and the room is suddenly empty. There is no sense of eyes any more. Tears flood my own eyes my face my mouth sobs catch in my throat I long for freedom but no freedom is to be found anywhere.

He does not untie me. I am red raw I am burning I am choking on tears but he does not untie me.

Instead so slow so cold so hard so unyielding! the handle of the crop is slid into the waiting arching body while something cold hard and rigid is slipped into the other orifice which waits oh how it waits for something to happen.

The crop handle slides in and out, wet with my juices, ribbed enough to cause screaming sensations the screaming of the pain of thrashed cheeks screaming of the pain of suppressed desire explode as I writhe and scream and yell my orgasm aloud.

Lauren sat shaking, trembling from head to foot, nipples hard, clitoris aching, vulva begging.

Tomorrow I'll phone and ask about that job. Tomorrow I'll go walking in Fleet Street, in hope of finding a new job and a new man.

I cannot go on like this.

I cannot go on alone.

I need a Master.

CHAPTER 3
AUGUST 1869

My dear Sister,

Oh how I wish I could send this letter to you! I wish I could sit with you and ask you how dear Mama is and how angry Papa is, and how the baby is and the little ones, and the pony and the dog and -

My heart is breaking with homesickness, dear Sophie, for all that there is life and bustle and excitement in this great city. It is that no one notices me! At home I was someone to be looked at, people - no, be honest - men turned as I passed, if the sun shone on my curls and in my eyes and if I tugged at my top just a little so my bosom showed and if I avoided a puddle with my skirts in my hand they would turn and I would feel the heat -

Here I am no one.

Here there are women who are so beautiful they would charm the summer nesting birds from the trees, stop the bees from entering the hive, reduce the wild flowers to mere weeds!

Women who touch their faces with powder and rouge, ah the forbidden things, sister! and who touch their bodies with perfume - and no doubt have every secret of washing with morning dew and rising with the lark and going to bed with the men who ask them -

If Papa were here among these brazen women and saw me lusting after the powder and rouge, the curls and the perfume he would give me more than the 60 strokes I had there in the church, tied the bench. It would be Papa and me alone and I would have to lean over the bench without restraint and take perhaps 100 strokes - ah sister, that would be punishment to avoid at all cost! So why do I linger on the thought?

Yet I do so yearn for the powder and rouge! And the curls, oh the curls, to have someone make my dancing wayward curls stand up in a bunch atop my head, and then to put on a hat - and I do so yearn for a man to stay the night. I am lonely at night, and seek night time company.

Does my dear sister see the root of the problem here?

Of all the people who stood on the platform that day in the sunshine in the dust and heat of our village station, of all the men who wore their whiskers with pride and their large bodies with wealth and their thoughts concealed behind their bland faces, I picked a man who does not like women.

Now I do not mean to say he does not LIKE women, he does. Albert Lymardson entertains women, delicate expensive women, but for a few friends who are not his way inclined.

Does this offend your startled little violet eyes, my sister? Men do like other men in a way that is not natural to us women to appreciate. And it shocked me too. I sat in my room alone a long long time, I stared at the guttering candle as it fought the pool of wax, I watched as moths clung to the flame and died, their wings shrivelled as the peelings thrown on the fire every morning are shrivelled and I cried and I cried because I wanted to come home.

For these are things I did not understand. And in not understanding I longed for things I knew and understood and felt at home with - you, our room, our pets and our fields, not huge buildings and stony streets and men who ignore me and men who did not respond to the swirl of a skirt, a flash of breasts, the twinkle of a female eye.

A lady found me alone. Someone entered the sanctuary I call my room, where hooks do for dressers and a table does for a cabinet and the bed is narrow and hard and I lay alone at night.

One of the silken ladies came in, drifting on shoes that whispered their leather secrets, with perfume that floated like a cloud of summer mist and voice that tinkled like the running water over stones.

"Why cry, my little one?" and the touch was like that of a butterfly fighting out of the web. She the spider coming closer and closer. I felt it was wrong, my sister, to have a woman in my room. As wrong as Alfred laying a hand on another man's arm and whispering in his ear and sharing a joke across the table, a joke that I felt shut me out.

Believe me, nothing improper is ever said before me! Nothing that I could write down for you and you would see what it is that offends me, it is there in the atmosphere in the look in the tone in the way they are with one another.

And it was making me fear for my future.

Now came this woman, Serenia, into my room. She locked the door with a flick of the lock and sat down on the bed so I could not but move toward her for the mattress did dip and tip me toward her side. And she caught me up in her arms and held me close.

"Why tears, my little one?" and I sobbed into her arms.

"I am afeared of Alfred and the men he is with and I am that lonely!"

"Ah, I see, fresh from the country, not understanding our London ways. Well, now - "she tipped up my chin and let me look into her eyes - "many of us like different things, my little one. I have desires too, and ones that will not go away, but we will explore them later, you and I. Before then, listen to me. Alfred is a good man. He took you in when you sought sanctuary, he will not turn you out, no matter what. You are useful to him, and that most valuable of things, a good loyal servant, and his friends like you. Be not afraid that they seem different. They, like me, have their own desires. Now, is that better?" and I nodded, for it was.

She touched my hand, my arm, my face and her touch was so gentle I could have cried again. "There is a desire I have which must be fulfilled, and Alfred has given me freedom to come and fulfil it with you. He said - correct me if I am wrong - that you will do anything to stay here in London, for you might be homesick but your heart is not in the country, is it?"

"No, it isn't." I said it carefully for fear of letting the accent show too much. But I must have let it show a little for she laughed and tugged my curls and said

"My pretty little yokel! Now, let us be clear with one another. I have a desire to spank a posterior good and hard, and yours is inviting a hand and a whip, would that I had a whip with me! And then my desire is to have you naked in your bed."

She must have read the shock on my face, for she added: "Alfred has told me of the thrashing you took from your church elders, for he knew it would interest me. It did more than that, it inflamed me. Come now, tell me, was it not a singular experience? Did you not long for the sting of the strap even as it fell? Did you not gladly let the men feast their eyes on the cheeks reddening under the punishment?"

Sister, it was as if she had looked into my heart, for these things I have turned over time and again in my mind in the loneliness of the night, when the watch calls "3 of the clock and all's well!" and I hear the tap of a passing stick and the clash of hooves as late night persons go about their business. I do not know if the

Watch do walk in other parts of this city, but here they do, in this Square the watch come around and tell the hour for the men here do like the assurance that all is well in the great city of London!

And I do listen for the man each night, and be assured all is well, even as I lay afeared for my future.

"Tell me about it" and her hand pressed down on mine and her eyes looked into mine.

So I told her how Papa locked me into the church and how I was afraid of the monsters and the corpses under the gravestones and the bats which flickered and she shuddered and smiled and said "I would have been too" which made me feel much assured.

And then I said how the elders came and stood and stared at me, and how the bench was brought and Papa pushed me down on it, how my limbs were tied and my pantaloons stripped off. And as I talked Serenia laid me down on my bed and pushed me over and I talked to the pillow, away from her all seeing eyes. I talked of how my skin felt cool in the cold church and she slipped aside my clothing so I was cool to the night air and her hand was soft and cool as it cupped my cheeks and separated them and explored the delicate skin and the tiny hole which thrilled at her finger tip touch. And as I talked of the strap landing ten times so she smacked me ten times with her hand which seemed so soft and yet stung so much and I talked on, of how the next ten were harder than before, and her ten were harder than before, hard hard smacks which rang around the tiny room and I shuddered and she said "Be still!" in a voice that took no argument from me.

And I told of the further ten which hurt much much more and how strong the arms were which held the strap and she gave me ten more, five on each cheek low nasty smacks and she waited while I talked on and smacked me again and again.

"But my smacks are nothing to the strapping you had" she told me, pulling me round so I sat up, my bottom blazing with her smacks, the skin on fire. And with a pull she had me over her knees, her silken knees, and her arm around my waist and I was pulled close to her and on display and I thrilled at her eyes looking at me and heard the indrawn breath and then she took up a leather slipper from her foot and spanked me with it over and over and around and I kicked and fought and struggled but her arm was stronger than my will to escape.

And then, oh my sister (I write these things only because I am sure your eyes will never read these words!) she laid me down again, so gentle in her arms, so loving, and kissed my lips with her powdered ones, and explored my tongue with hers and her hands were on my breasts and at my thighs and at my secret place and I gave way under her touch and I -

Sister of mine, I loved her.

"I am virgin still" I told her later, when the passion was done, when she had found my secret and shameful place with her tongue and her fingers, and I had found hers, and taken in the scent and the smell and the taste of her.

"I know. We will do something about that" and she rose swiftly and left me.

"Come back!" I cried. She looked and smiled and was gone. But in a moment she was back, bringing with her a young man I had not noticed at dinner. He must have come later.

"Here, a virgin for you, Cornelius." She gestured to me and sat down on the end of the bed. "My dear, this is Cornelius, a man who loves small and delicate ladies like yourself and who will take your maidenhead with all the skill a man can bring, but first you must make us both happy. Cornelius has brought the whip I so desired."

"Not on her back, my dear Serenia, such a delicate lady should not be whipped on her back." His voice was as dark as he was, and as handsome.

"No no!" she laughed and clapped her hands, the whip between them. "No, the posterior, Cornelius, which I have spanked bright red already with much pleasure and a good deal of satisfaction. This is what I needed to complete the feast."

I did not move.

They lifted me from the bed, bent me over the end so my body stuck up in the air and Cornelius sat and held my wrists firm in his hands, so white, the nails so well trimmed and cared for, not like the hands of the rough men in our village, dear sister! These are gentlemen after all. And Serenia brought that whip across my backside ten times, and I screamed out at every one, for the lash cut me in a way I had never had before, so different from the strap, so different from her hand, so different from Papa's switch and birch! I fought Cornelius' hand but he never let me go, and I had to take them, every lash, across the backside so sore from her spanks!

And then Cornelius lifted me, laid me down and put my legs over his shoulders and entered me. He was large and smooth and wet already and my backside was burning and hurting and tears cascaded down my face. I felt him slide and push and slide and push and the whole shameful thing my whole secret place gave way to take him in. A rush of feeling came over me so intense, so wild so unbelievable I clawed at his shoulders and his back and his ears and his arms and what I could get hold of and he thrust and thrust and -

One sharp pain and I was maiden no more, sister.

And in the losing of the maidenhead I found the rush that was passion. I knew this is what Peter James should have taken but didn't. I am right glad it were this man, this expert man with his ways and this woman with her hand and her whip that brought me to it, for I understood that it was the pain which made the pleasure so good.

How I should know such things I cannot be saying but it is true.

And sister, I will do it again.

And again.

And no longer do I cry for hayricks and open fields, for lambs and cows, for birds and foxes stalking around the chicken houses, for I have found my place in the great City even if it be no more than to offer my body for pain and pleasure to those who wish to take it of me and from me.

For there were gold coins to pay for the maidenhead and the whipping, the slippering which left me sore and crying brought me money.

And it brought me passion.

And sister, what more could I ask than that?

CHAPTER 4

As Lauren entered the building she felt it reach out and enfold her. She had never been there before, never thought of going into Fleet Street before, let alone this dark undistinguished doorway, yet she knew the way the stairs curved, knew which ones to avoid as they would creak, knew how the doors sat in the walls, entryways to everything.

Reeves Marmon & Co. were on the 3rdfloor. The painted frosted glass door welcomed her, surely once it had been oak panelled and solid? But no matter. She pushed it open and went in.

A large room awaited her, a desk tucked in the left hand corner held switchboard, paperwork, baskets, and a junior with a bright smiling face. Beyond her, three desks, girls typing away busily, earphones in ears, pretending to be oblivious to the newcomer.

"Can I help you?"

"I have an appointment with Mr Hazelton. Lauren Sanderson, interview for the secretary's job."

"Right, just a moment." The girl picked up the phone and pressed a button.

"Thank you." Lauren swung the shoulder bag firmly on to her shoulder, wished her hands would stop sweating, and looked around. It was a typical Solicitors' office, cluttered, untidy, coffee jar and tea bags on the mantel along with a shiny electric kettle and cups, an opened packet of biscuits and a few law books. Across the other side of the room the almost floor to ceiling window looked out on the facade of a City church and the rooftops of the City. Below there would be be rushing vans and people, hustle and bustle. Temple was a million miles from here.

"Come this way." The corridor was narrow, marked with lines here and there where people had rubbed against the walls. The carpet was worn yet still of good quality, the suite of offices as a whole had a solid olde worlde quality about them that in her mind typified a good solicitors' office.

Lauren walked across half a mile of carpet to a huge desk fronted by two chairs. The room was bright, cheerful, decorated with plants, heavy law books and a bright sense of purpose and polish.

"Mr Hazelton, I'm Lauren Sanderson." She shook hands with the short tubby man with the huge smile and friendly eyes.

"Thank you for answering the ad." He lowered himself into a huge winged chair and tilted it back. "Unfortunately I've since filled the post for my secretary, but tell me about yourself and your experience anyway."

Why? she wondered, but then thought, why not? He might have some other ideas.

"Well I'm 25, single, live alone, and I started work in law in a small firm just off Gracechurch Street at the age of 15. I was junior and runabout, you know the sort of thing, progressed to secretary, and stayed there three years. We did all sorts there, litigation mostly. After that I went for six weeks with a firm who did Admiralty law. I only stayed six weeks because they took two girls on when they really only needed one, and I had nothing to do. One day I only typed six letters! So I left, and went to a firm in Leadenhall Street where I did company work, marriage settlements, all that kind of thing. Then I got a job locally, where I did conveyancing, debt collection, petty crime, you know how it is. That lasted for a year or so, but then I wanted to come back to London, I missed the bustle of the City and got a job helping two young solicitors set up a practice right behind here, in Temple. They're successfully running now, so the excitement has gone, and I'd like another change."

"You have a lot of experience to bring to the job," he observed, steepling his fingers and putting them under his chin, his eyes still twinkling but watchful. "But you tend to move around a lot. If you came here, do you think you would stay?"

"That depends on a lot of things." She went for open honesty. "I would like to stay somewhere, I'd like to be happy enough not to be looking for a move all the time. You're in the exciting part of the City, I could enjoy walking around here during the lunch hour! If the work is demanding and interesting, then yes, I probably would. I only have one commitment, I work part time as a Private Investigator, and occasionally have to go to Court to give evidence."

"I'm sure we could accommodate that. But as I said, I have a secretary now. After I placed the ad, the lady who was working as a temp has decided to stay. But - " before Lauren could protest, he interrupted her. "My Legal Executive, Judith Brooke does need a secretary. If you're interested, if you don't mind working for a woman, I'll take you through to meet her. I think you two would go well together."

"I can work with a woman." Lauren surprised herself by saying that. The women she had met in the legal profession had been bitches, but somehow the words, like the been-here-before feeling on entering, were the right thing to say, the right thing to do.

She got up as Mr Hazelton did, followed him to the door, preceded him into the corridor, and then allowed him to go back along the corridor, past the room full to the ceiling with dead filed tied with the ubiquitous pink tape, and into another smaller room.

"Judith, this is Lauren Sanderson, came for the interview, but you know Stella Thompson has decided to stay on so - "

"I need someone so you brought her in here. Good idea." The voice came deep, almost manly, from the woman behind the desk. She stood up, a firm solid figure with full breasts and full hips, iron grey hair and an engaging smile that matched the blue eyes. The hand she held out was unlined, firm, with unpainted nails and solid gold rings. Somehow it all fitted the image. She wore a white blouse under a black jacket matched with a full red skirt, making Lauren feel dowdy almost instantly. Judith Brooke wore her clothes with pride, that was a fact.

"I'll leave you two to talk it over" and he was gone. Lauren sat down, admired the painting on the wall, a fine delicate water colour, and then looked out of the window. The view was the same as the one from the typists' room, obviously this was alongside that room.

"My secretary gave notice just yesterday." Judith Brooke swivelled around in her chair, toyed with a pen, slightly nervous, and yet Lauren could have sworn she'd be full of determination and stolid self assurance. Perhaps there was a touch of femininity underneath to offset the bold exterior. Lauren felt herself warming to the woman immediately as she continued. "I don't like starting over with someone new, but it happens." Judith leaned forward. "I do all the divorce work around here, I don't suppose Mike Hazelton told you that, but I do. It means some traumatic stuff at times, sexual abuse, violence, are you familiar with all that?"

"I work as a part time Private Investigator."

"That says it all." Judith Brooke leaned back, looked at Lauren with calculating eyes. "Would you be prepared to give that up if I asked?"

"Yes." The response was immediate and almost automatic. Lauren wondered at herself.

"Good. I won't ask you yet, but I may do. However, that's for later. I like you. Tell me about your experience." Once again Lauren found herself going through her history, and the reasons why she had left each job. At the same time a corner of her mind wondered over and over again why she agreed so suddenly and so completely to give up the job which meant money and security to her because one person had asked.

"Fine, I think we can work together. What do you think? The salary is acceptable to you?"

"Yes, it is." Lauren stood as Judith did, shook hands over the desk, the smile deepening. "It sounds good. I'll go and give my notice in now, and I'll be here Monday week, if that's all right."

"Fine. We'll confirm it in writing, of course." She moved toward a different door.

"I look forward to starting work with you," said Lauren as she followed, and she meant it.

"Everyone, this is Lauren Sanderson, she's coming to work for me Monday week." Earphones were removed, faces turned to Lauren with interest and friendly smiles. Judith shook Lauren's hand again. "If you'll leave your address with Linda - "

"Sure."

"I'll see you Monday week" and with a swirl of red skirt Judith was gone, the door closing firmly behind her. The girl opposite Lauren smiled.

"Welcome to the madhouse. I'm Jenny, Judith's secretary as was, the reason you got a job."

"Don't you like it here or something?" Lauren asked, smiling back.

The girl shook her head. "I love it. Judith's a great person to work for, but I'm having a baby."

"Congratulations!" Lauren moved over to leave her address with the girl, and turned back again. "See you all next week. Best of luck!" she added, throwing the words in Jenny's direction.

"Thanks! Enjoy the job!"

Lauren felt the building nod almost in approval as she left the office, and began to walk down the stairs again, trailing a hand down the worn bannister.

I know this place. It feels right, it feels comfortable to me. I shall be happy here.

But why did I agree to give up my part time job?

In a sudden blinding flash of light Lauren knew why she had agreed, knew too that Judith Brooke would ask her to give up the job at some time, and would possibly ask her to do a lot of other things too.

She was a dominant, and Lauren had automatically submitted to her will.

Instead of searching out an interesting male face on the underground train, Lauren gave herself over to looking for a woman, a dominant strong woman, one like Judith. Just for a change, she told herself, I'll have a different fantasy tonight. And I need one. She had given her boss the bad news of her departure, saw his crestfallen face, almost changed her mind, but back behind her crowded desk knew there was no way she could go on working there. A sudden memory of the large sunlit airy office, with its view of the sky and rooftops, and more particularly, of the powerful personality of Judith Brooke, intruded and added weight to her decision to go.

Then she had phoned the Detective Agency, spoken to Ray Barker, asking if there was work for her, to find there was nothing she could handle. Tonight again she would be alone with thoughts and desires, a night with a fantasy and perhaps the added thrill of a second vibrator for change - that would be very good. Very good.

It was going to be fairly easy to give up the part time work if Judith asked, because there had been less and less work lately, whether by accident or design. Maybe Ray was crowding her out - in which case, she would be glad to go. The thought of never having to go out in dark winter evenings again, never have to drive around looking for streets, houses, people who did not want to be found, that would be heaven.

Yes, Lauren decided, I'm about ready to give up the part time job. The moment she asks me.

And then she saw a Judith lookalike, a tall well built woman with impeccable clothes, a suit that fitted everywhere, looked stylish looked fashionable and expensive. Her hair was dark where Judith's was grey, but the look was the same, the 'I own everything here' look that meant people got out of her way.

As she left the train at the stop before Lauren's, Lauren sent thoughts after her, are you a dominant woman? Would you like me to visit you?

She got up as the train pulled into her own station, hurried out of the crowded concourse, and found her little grey car, still needing its wash and service, and drove home. For once she was able to ignore the seedy look of the mobile home park, for once she was not afraid of the loneliness of the tiny unit tucked in the corner.

The July evening was sticky and close. Lauren set a kettle to boil on the small calor gas stove, praying the gas wouldn't run out. She hastily ate a sandwich and drank a glass of orange, and then poured the kettle of water into the sink. She closed the small flimsy curtain, locked the door of the unit, and stripped off, throwing her clothes into the bedroom ready for washing later.

Then she began to wash, sliding a sponge carefully under silk smooth arms, around full breasts with their large nipples and gentle weight resisting the sponge, appreciating the warm water. Across rounded belly, around hips, sliding in to the quim, tousling the curled bristly hair, parting her thighs, letting the water drip between her legs, mopping away the juices which had run at the thought of a fantasy tonight. Between her cheeks, slow, sure, drawing the water round like a lover's hand. The length of a leg, the touch of her feet, the raspy roughness and pleasure of the towel, the sprinkling of perfumed talc to counteract the mustiness of the kitchen.

And then she laid flat on the bed, gazing up at the water stained ceiling, clutching the vibrators, one white and slim and feeling as if it was pulsing with power in her right hand, the other small and discreet. She parted her legs, gripped a nipple between two fingers, and began to fantasise.

I am walking along the road, an address in my mind, aware of being on time, for surely you must be on time to visit a mistress.

Here, this is the house, with neat railings and manicured garden, with beautifully cared for wooden door and glittering brass knocker and letter box. This is it. My nemesis my pain my dues.

My fluttering nerves can surely be heard a hundred yards away! The dryness of my mouth, the dampness of my palms, the wetness of my quim, oh why am I walking here, what am I doing here, what is the matter with me? Walking toward pain. It would make a good title for an erotic book. If I had the time to write it.

The door opens as if by magic, why do I always assume - forget it concentrate here touch here under the breast here, where the cheek curves toward the thigh so soft so real so - feminine. Touch myself feel the lips quiver feel their wrinkled wetness feel their sensitivity how easy it would be to hurt myself to press to squeeze to send pain shivering through me. What would it be like to be pierced there, to have someone pull on the ring, to have something attached to the ring, weights, - oh feel the flutter of feelings as I feel myself! Oh sense the sensations squirming through me as I slowly stroke myself with the throbbing vibrator.!

She is there, my mistress. The lady from the train. She is wearing a simple white dress, no sleeves, low cut showing her ample shapely breasts. The dress clings, I see the outline of her hips, the sweep of bone into the pelvic region, the cluster of curls at her mound, and I long to touch to caress to taste but no, that is not why I am here. Why I am here is a different thing entirely.

"Come" and I follow, for I always do in my fantasies and I do in real life, I follow.

A dungeon. A playroom, she calls it, a room with padded benches and horses to bend over, straps for suffering and a mirror to see. And racks of implements of pain and pleasure awaiting my skin my skin my skin.

With one swift fluid movement my mistress strips off the white dress and stands in silver bikini skintight and concealing nothing. Her nipples are erect at the thought of dealing with me. She detests men yet deals with them daily, for money. She treats them like the dirt she considers they are, women for her are a pleasure and they come free. In disciplining women she finds her pleasure, and she brings all her skills to the punishment sessions.

Over her knees, her cool skin on mine, for I am stripped to nothing to be sure she misses no part of me she wishes to hurt. Over her knees feeling childish and waiting for the sting of whatever she chooses, never her hands, her white hands with the glittering red nails are not allowed to touch someone, she prefers to use something hard and inflexible usually. Now, a paddle. Flat and hard, it covers a wide area, it smacks on this cheek and that and I gasp and writhe and she orders me to be still and I am. Again and again, the paddle, flat hard unyielding, crushes the flesh stings the skin raises redness and sharp stinging pain that makes me gasp and cry out and disobey the order to be still.

Over a padded bench, hands secured to the legs, ankles secured to each other, helpless, cannot balance, must lean forward, must throw the body weight into the bench as she has designed it to do. Helpless. Bottom red and stinging, helpless I await the tawse, her favourite, a three tailed heavy one that is well used, flexible, well able to deliver a violent and nasty sting, as it does now. Twelve from one side, twelve from the other. I know the drill, she has done it before. Twelve times standing to my right, the thickness of the leather and delight of the leather wrapping itself around me covering both cheeks at once, covering the stinging redness of the paddle, covering my skin, I cry out for release and yet delight in the pain, for the pain goes deep and touches every erotic feeling I have. Thrills and spills thrill of anticipation and apprehension of fear and longing and spill of juices which are oozing and she knows it.

She stands, I get twelve strokes from her standing to my left, the leather wrapping itself over the weals already inflicted, I am crying out and protesting and getting nowhere for the twelve will come whether I want it or not, and I do want it, of course I do, it is my desire, my feeling, my own decision to be there.

I am allowed to rest and wait to stand and to rub and to ease the pain a little before the cane, oh twelve hard nasty cuts with a fine whippy cane are enough and then and then and then -

The vibrator in Lauren's slit, deep, deep, throbbing, the small one, hand rolling around the lips, touching the clit with the buzzing angry head thrusting deep deep inside slick with wetness, slick with her wetness, in and out again, rolling around and around, one vibrator here, one vibrator there, buzzing, throbbing, touching, sliding down the inner thighs, back around the hair, touching tormenting teasing, finding the clit again bringing it erect in its tiny hood touching and sliding, ramming deep deep inside again and back out and around, touching and sliding and buzzing and awakening until the feelings rush toward the great climax - the vibrator buzzes silently inside touching all the nerves all the nerves all the nerves -

Outside a lawn mower sang its song of destruction. Inside Lauren lay still, sweating again, exhausted and smiling. Somewhere along the way the woman from the train had transformed into Judith Brooke.

Only a week and a half to go and she would be working for Judith Brooke.

CHAPTER 5

My dear Sister,

Looking back at the letter which I have not sent - and how my heart aches not to send them to you! I see that I have not anywhere told you about Alfred Lymardson, dear Alfred, who rescued me that awful day on the village station when my heart was full and my body ached with bruises!

Alfred is a fine man, tall, strong with broad shoulders that well fit a smoking jacket or well cut tweed, his broad chest supports well the gold chain, the silver cravat and the sateen waistcoats he so admires. He wears dark whiskers that curl around his face, so delicate, so fine boned he could be a woman. He does not work in the way Papa and the elders of our village would know work, he does nothing with his hands, which are white and fair and well manicured and handsome as he is. His main means of earning a living is to gamble.

Ah, see how your dear sister has fallen among the fallen! Such depravity, such sin! Such unwholesome goings on, such spawn of the Devil! How Papa's phrases and sermons on fire and brimstone come back to haunt me at night when the candle burns low and the voices drift up from beneath me to my narrow bed, voices of wealth, of culture, of impeccable breeding! The slap of cards, the clink of coin, the raised voices when another loses, for Alfred do win, more times than not, large sums of money.

Rarely does Alfred lose, and how we in the household do shudder and hide when Alfred loses! For then the doors shake and the chandelier tinkles in its setting. He goes roaring around the house slamming this and picking on that, and all who get in his way are bellowed at and shrieked at. I have yet to experience Alfred's hands on me, but one day I will, if I be in the wrong place at the wrong time. I did believe he hit no woman, but last week he did get the new 'tween maid Dominica and beat her around the legs for showing her ankles, beat her with a stick he took from the hall and did hurt her sore bad!

I would have put myself in her place and took the beating for her, being well used to the feel of the strap and stick now after these weeks of living in Alfred's house - something I will tell you later, dear sister - but I could not come between them for he shouted at me to be gone.

Why Alfred did take on so I did not know, until Cornelius did tell me one night in one of his visits - again something I will tell you later, dear sister - that Alfred had money aplenty from an inheritance. It was the losing, the blow to his pride, which was shaming, and caused the tempers.

It is eight weeks since I came to live in Alfred's house.

We are a small household, there is Cook, Mrs Evadne Gorton, who is long since a widow and who knows Mr Alfred's needs backwards. It is whispered by some that she was once Nanny to Mr Alfred (she calls him that) when he was a baby and certainly looks old enough for that! From talk I believe this much to be true, that she then married and moved into Hampstead village but soon became a widow due to a bull that run amok and he (Mr Gorton) rescued a child from its path only to be gored himself. So she came back to Mr Alfred and eventually became his Cook.

And there is Lizzy who comes to do the heavy wash and to scuttle about doing the heavy work, gets in the coal and cleans the grates ready for new fires and who scrubs the kitchen floor and sweeps the yard and sees to Mr Alfred's dirty boots.

There is Briggs, a stable man and driver of the carriage Mr Alfred keeps to go about his calls. Briggs has a look which says he would bed me but I keep away from him for Cook says he is a rough man with rough tastes and goes with low women. I do not want to catch anything from such a man. I see him at the times when we meet at the kitchen table for breakfast for dinner and for supper, for Alfred is generous with his staff and I eat well, my sister, better than I did at home when Papa would dictate we were to give everything up for Lent and other festivals. Alfred says there are no days we give up anything, or so Cook says!

And to help with the work and the serving and the seeing to the guests - Mr Alfred has so many! - there is Dominica, a new 'tween maid who does a lot of hurrying about.

And of them all I feel I am the only one to have the power - because I can say No when Serenia or Cornelius come to my room, it is within my power to say no. I know because I push the boundaries just a little, sometimes I say to Serenia

"No please not the slipper tonight" and she will say

"All right, then I will use the strap, does that suit your Ladyship?" and I know she is pleasing me.

For all they came to me first, I choose to let them go on coming. I could have gone to Alfred and said "This I do not wish to have" and he would have stopped them for he said one morning -

"But say the word, Clarisse, and the visits will stop," and I said

"No Alfred, for you they will continue and for me, for I do enjoy them."

"By God, 'tis well I picked you up that day!" he said and went back to The Times.

I know without saying not to mention my desires to any but Serenia and Cornelius, for the others do look at me in a different way, when Alfred calls me over, adjusts my dress, exposes my bosom and ruffles up my curls. Then I see their eyes on me and know their thoughts. But Alfred did whisper to me one morning when the mood was good and the papers told Good News and the winnings were high that Serenia and Cornelius were good friends of his, the only ones who shared the feeling of domination, and that was the first time I had heard the word from his lips, sister. So I knew to be quiet to the others.

Serenia comes to my room many a night, sometimes when the bruises are not yet gone. Sometimes she comes alone, and we would be lovers, after I had admitted my sins to her, thoughts I had, things I had dropped, such casual trivial things but which warranted a time over her knees being punished with all manner of things, from her soft white hand which stung even though it were so soft and white! and her slipper and my slipper and a strap which she loves to use, one affixed to a wooden handle, a short piece of leather which slaps and bites and hurts and makes me yelp aloud so much that Serenia would laugh as she beats me with it. For sure she loves that strap! It do sting and dance its way across my cheeks to the tune of her smiles and her chuckles and I squirm and wriggle and yelp and kick and make a fuss for the thing do burn and hurt but after, oh after when the glow begins to spread, when the pain settles to stinging and then to glowing, then the feeling is like nothing on earth. And if at that moment Serenia do have her mouth at my purse and her tongue at my spot taking up my juices -

Then, sister, my cheeks and back leave the bed and I do thrust myself at her face and her mouth and I do spread my legs and cry out for sheer pleasure of it.

And then I do for Serenia what she has done for me.

But then comes the night when Cornelius do come with her and then I find I shake in my shoes.

Cornelius is what I think of as a true Man, unlike Alfred, Cornelius is a dark man with dark hair and dark visage and dark dark eyes that smoulder with passion when he looks at me and knows I have done wrong. Sometimes he is at dinner, and watches every move I make when serving, and makes me nervous, so time and time again I spill a drop of wine or tilt a spoon of soup too far, or stumble on the way to the dresser. Sometimes he is not at dinner but comes later, when they are at cards, and I hear his steps on the stairs, his form step, his deep voice, his low laughter compared to Serenia's high musical laugh.

Then do I shake because Cornelius is a hard man. When he comes, it is either standing still, hands above my head or on my head, body stretched out and his small whip or crop across my back and cheeks, sometimes drawing blood and I am not to make a sound. With Serenia I can make a fuss if I choose, if the strap stings too much -

And dear sister the strap always stings too much! and I wonder how many times you have felt Papa's strap since I ran away - how many times you have been summonsed to the study, there to have a litany of sins read out against you, and to bend over the chair and lift your skirts and have Papa deal out a measured dose of the strap on your small round cheeks, so much smaller than mine, for you are altogether so much thinner than I ever was. Papa used to say that I had a fullness that could be well beaten and he did beat me well!

But I digress. Cornelius comes and says

"I saw you spill the wine, spill the soup, stumble with the silver platter, come here" and I know I am to suffer punishment for the errors. But his presence makes me commit errors, because of his eyes ever watchful on me!

He says he is punishing me because Alfred will not and cannot and someone has to discipline the servants. But I do not hear him go to Dominica or Cook or Lizzy who comes early and leaves at night having sometimes only polished half the grate or leaves the front door knocker! Why is it only me, the poor little girl who has no home, who is punished?

Because I am the only one who likes it.

Cornelius punishes me in a way Serenia never does. With Serenia it is always to go across her knees in a love embrace, her arm around me, her closeness thrilling me, her perfume, her skin her musk all is good to me. With Cornelius it is distant, it is standing and waiting and feeling the lash of the crop or the bite of the birch - yes, once he made up a birch and birched me long and hard! And it is his pleasure I make not a sound, but take it as if I am willing to take it. By silence I show I accept.

And then Serenia leaves my room, closes the door and leaves Cornelius to toss me to the bed and fuck me. Oh sister, the word will offend, but it is only the word, his cock is so hard so strong so sure which thrusts in and out, which slides in wetness and passion, which touches every part of me and which thrills every part of me through to my brain for sure my brain explodes when he does and I do, with my legs fair wrapped around that hard waist and those hard muscles, the legs that pulse with his thrusts and the purse which gives oh it gives to his manliness!

And always the gold coins are left on the table as they leave, whether it be Serenia or Cornelius, gold coins are always there. And sometimes I long to say

"I would do this for love of you!" but know that one day my luck may turn even as Alfred's luck may turn and I may find myself out on the street with no one and nothing to care for me, so I must of means take care of myself. So sister I hoard my coins in a safe place, and one day I shall be bold and take them to a Bank and put them safe on deposit as I hear Alfred talk of doing with his monies when he has won.

I have a dream which I can tell only to paper for fear of those who would laugh at me. I dream of owning my own home and having girls there who love the sting of the strap as I do, and have people come to give them that strap, people who love it as Serenia does. For in Society such things are not talked of, and there must be those who are longing in their heart to use a strap on someone hard and long, to see the flesh on the buttocks turn red and then redder and then deepest red as the strap bites and raises the pain that surges through the body.

And I would choose my own lovers, as all who submit to the strap do choose if they are of free and strong will.

Ah dreams! But as the gold mounts up beneath my bed, my sister, I can see the dream come closer and closer!

The candle burns low, about to drown in its own pool of wax even as I am drowning in the pool of my own juices, for tonight Serenia was hard with the strap and I am exhausted.

I know one thing, my sister, my lovers will not be men.

CHAPTER 6
AUGUST 1969

Another rumble of thunder rolled across the city sky, followed almost immediately by another blinding flash of lightening. Lauren paused, fingers on the keyboard, wondering if the power would hold out. She had a long and very important set of papers to type, and the storm was increasing in severity. Rain lashed the large windows, stormed down drainpipes, raced along gutters and overflowed. The church opposite streamed tears.

"I don't like storms." Linda shivered in her corner, almost cowering over the switchboard.

"We'll be all right." Liz, the other secretary, looked up from her intensive study of a file and frowned. "But we are on the 3rdfloor - " As if in answer to her doubts, another bolt of lightning thrust itself violently through the room, crackling and sparking. The lights went out the moment the thunder followed, filling the room with sound, shaking the windows, smothering for the first time the sound of the traffic outside. Liz and Stella shrieked in unison, Linda yelped and sat on the floor. Lauren looked around her in quiet desperation and frustration. There was so much to do, and now her means of doing it had been taken away from her by a force she could not control. It was slightly frightening, the intensity of the storm, the power of the rain.

Judith put her head round the door and smiled at Lauren through the depths of the gloom that crept beneath the ink-filled clouds outside..

"Is it too dark to type?"

Lauren nodded. "I might just manage, but there's no power anyway."

"Well, how about doing some filing in my office?"

"Sure." Glad to have something to do other than sit and listen to hysterical outbursts from Linda and the others each time the lightning flashed, Lauren scooped up a pile of letters and carried them into the room. "You can be signing these while we can't do anything else."

"Damn storm, I wanted those papers done."

"I know. I'll stay late and finish them."

"Would you?" Judith's frown creased into a smile. "That's good of you."

"No, it's not, you've been good to me. Since I've been here I've had time off for court appearances and for dentist, I owe you one. And anyway, there's nothing to go home to."

She began flipping through the filing, picking up papers, letters, carbons, memos, opening and closing the filing cabinet drawers with as much caution as she could. Metal filing cabinets did tend to clang and Judith often had blinding headaches.

"Do you have a boy friend, Lauren?"

She turned in surprise. Judith hadn't mentioned anything personal in the month Lauren had been there, even though at times there had been a desperate tension about Judith, a set in the lips, a look in the eyes, an unhappiness that almost radiated from her.

Lauren leaned against the filing cabinet, papers in her arms, looking at her boss in the dimness of the darkening sky and the flashes of lightning. Rain poured down the window, a background to the raging storm and her own raging emotions.

"No. I had one, a serious live-in partner, but - we split about three or four months back now." A roll of thunder crashed across the roof, shaking everything.

"Tell me about it,"

"Well I found out - after guessing of course - that he'd been seeing other women, a lot of them in fact!

He found some erotic books I had, used them as an excuse to call me perverted and sick and stormed out. Three days later I had notice to quit our flat."

"I thought you had an odd address. It's a caravan park, isn't it?"

"Yes. Pretty awful, to be honest, all the decent homes are in the front where everyone sees them, mine's a tiny unit with outside loo and no bathroom, stuck in a corner. The rent's pretty cheap, so I suppose I have to put up with it - for now."

"What about the boy friend?"

"What about him?" Lauren tried to keep her tone light, but she could not take refuge in filing now, the room was too dark. To her surprise Judith opened the bottom drawer, pulled out a couple on candles and set them on the desk in saucers, lighting them with a flick of a match. The glow was softening, the mood intimate. Lauren put the filing in the basket and sat down. Another flash of lightning, but this time the thunder was delayed by a few seconds. The storm was moving on.

"I've had this scenario before, the power often goes off here if there's a storm, it's an old building, very fragile. Now, tell me, the boy friend?"

"Justin. What about him?"

"Do you miss him?"

"Yes and no. He wasn't much good to me, off with others, times I wanted him and he couldn't, that kind of thing."

"I know." The tone was so sad Lauren wanted to cry. "I've been having a bad time lately with my boy friend, I've just thrown him out. Listen." Judith sat up, away from the flames, into the semi darkness of the small room. "Why don't we go out one night and get tight together? You and me? And you can tell me about those erotic books your boy friend didn't like. Or do you want to tell me now?"

Lauren hesitated, felt her heart leap, felt herself drawn closer to this woman whom she had come to admire so much over the last four weeks, and said into the darkness

"They were s/m books."

There was a silence, and a creak of the chair. Then Judith stirred, smiled into the candlelight, went to say something - and the lights came back on, killing the intimate moment stone dead with brightness.

"I'll go get on with the papers." Lauren went quietly out of Judith's office, back to light and activity. Already typewriters were clicking, Stella Thompson, Mr Hazelton's new secretary, looking panicky as she tried to catch up with the work.

Lauren picked up the telephone. "Give me an outside line, Linda, would you? Thanks." She dialled the Agency. The answering machine cut in, and Ray's stiff unnatural voice came on. Lauren smiled as she waited for him to drone through his message, then spoke quickly.

"Ray, it's Lauren, whatever you have for me tonight, forget it. The storm caused a power cut, so I've got to work late to catch up. Call you tomorrow."

Outside the rain fell even harder, great torrents of water cascading out of dark overloaded clouds. Lauren had revealed a secret to a virtual stranger, something she never did. What had come over her?

The storm eased as the afternoon went on, the power stayed on, typewriters purred as they all worked steadily through the workload. Rain lessened and then stopped in time for Linda to rush to the Post Office and buy a new load of stamps and get the franking machine reloaded, and for Judith to go out on a mysterious errand, coming back with wet feet and a smug look. Lauren didn't ask where she'd been, just handed over the phone messages. And all the time she asked herself what Judith would make of the s/m revelation, would it be mentioned again, should she have said it, what effect did it have, really? If only the light hadn't come on! If only Judith had spoken!

Everyone left at 5.30, hustling out of the door, shouting goodbye to Lauren and bad luck at having to work. Lauren eased herself back in the chair, put her hands behind her neck and massaged the stiff muscles. It was going to be a long day, and tomorrow even longer, if this pile of work was anything to go by. Damn rescheduling by the Court!

"Break time." Judith appeared suddenly, plugged in the electric kettle, set cups out on the mantel. "It IS good of you to work late, Lauren, no matter what you say. I don't find many people prepared to give that kind of loyalty to a firm."

"I'm not giving it to the firm." Lauren spoke quickly, afraid she would falter over the words. "I'm giving it to you."

The statement lay on the carpet between them, sinking into the rough cord, mingling with the dust of the day.

The kettle began to bubble and hiss steam. Judith and Lauren stared at one another, Lauren looking at the grey waves round the firm yet beautiful face, noting the strong set of the jaw, the determined line of the lips, and in a flash wondered what it would be like to be over those knees, being spanked by those squared off firm hands, hands which handled clients with delicacy and office staff with a gentle authority, and Lauren with kid gloves.

Even though she had made some foolish mistakes. Judith had been kindness itself, just pointing them out and getting her do it over again.

When the kettle switched off, Judith made black coffees.

"Sorry, there's no milk left, it's designed to last until we all go home at 5.30 of course."

"I don't mind." Lauren took the cup, set it on her desk and waited, knowing there was more to come.

"Listen." There was more to come. Judith found a typist's chair, drew it close to Lauren's desk, put her cup down and looked at Lauren, meeting her eyes firmly and determinedly.

"I've been on an errand, but you're not yet to know what I've bought. I'm taking a huge leap in the dark here but I believe I'm going to land on the right piece of ground. Somehow I think I've about sized you up this last month. OK, this is what I propose, for starters anyway. I did say would you give up your job, I'm asking you to give it up."

"All right." It was as if another huge load had been taken from Lauren, rather like the feeling she had when she decided to phone for this job vacancy.

"I want you to give it up for one reason. Sometimes you may have to stay late."

"All right," Lauren repeated, still waiting, for she sensed there was more to come, a lot more.

"Now, what I'm about to say is strictly between us two. You have the choice of saying NO right now and I'll respect that, and if you do I'll never mention it again; but think about it before you do. The reason you may have to stay late sometimes is so you can be punished for mistakes."

A silence deep as anything Lauren had ever known sank over them. Judith waited, eyes glittering with emotion and tension. Lauren let her hands rest in her lap, felt the surge of feeling run through her, down her thighs, round her cheeks, into her pubis, tightening muscles, sending thrills up her spine until they connected with her brain, and then felt a cold cold swell go over her, a sense of apprehension, anticipation and pure sexual feeling.

Here was her chance to find out what it was really like without committing herself to someone rough, perhaps an over enthusiastic dominant who would push her too hard for her own good. Here was her chance - all she had to do was take it.

The moment stretched out, the silence palpable between them. Then Lauren raised her eyes, felt her mass of auburn hair shift and as always fall down over one eye. She pushed it back.

"All right."

Judith smiled, a deep knowing smile.

"Good. It's what I thought you'd say. Now, tell me, have you ever been spanked or disciplined in any way?"

"No, never, it's all in my head. It's all been a fantasy."

"Right. I'll go easy to start with, but we'll progress, won't we? Move from spankings to something harder, depending on how you react, how you get on, and how many mistakes you make!"

Judith stood up, wiped her hands down her skirt, hands which may have been sweaty with apprehension at Lauren's reaction, she didn't know, and walked away. Lauren watched the firm hips disappear into the office, looked at her own hands, which were shaking, and smiled.

What would Justin say if he knew?

Judith came back out, holding a small brown bag.

"Here, a present to read on the way home. The rest of my purchases I'm keeping here, and I'm keeping secret right now."

Lauren took the bag, put it in her own bag without looking at it, nodded, said thank you in a tiny voice, and slipped the earphones in again, determined to work.

It had felt like a book, an s/m book no doubt, one to replace those which Justin had destroyed. Something to give her ideas, something to give her an indication of what was to come.

The rest of Judith's purchases were something to speculate on, when she was flat on her bed with a vibrator in her hand and which she would find out soon enough.

CHAPTER 7
SEPTEMBER 1869

My dear Sister,

You would be so proud of me had you seen me today! Remember how as girls we would play at being grand ladies, pretending we had a carriage and pair and would step down outside our house and the door would be swept open for us -

Serenia had given me a dress, oh such a dress as you would never see in our small village! Such a high collar, such a skirt with flounces and frills to move around the feet as I walk! and high buttoned boots to go with it. Oh sister, it is blue as the skies over the downland, with lace as delicate as Spring clouds.

With my dark curls and my face, which you know, sister, is as oval as my mirror, and my dark eyes alight with excitement, I swear I looked the part of the fine lady!

One fine day and it was a fine day here in London, the sun shining clear and strong, the buildings washed with sun rays, and looking very elegant as befits a great capital city! I put aside my working dress of black and white, put aside the small apron and cap, and donned this fine blue dress. I put my curls up with combs, put a bonnet on top, brushed a touch of powder on my cheeks, oh yes, I have some powder too, I carefully spent a gold coin on some for myself! and put the rest of the coins in a small velvet pouch which I wore beneath my bodice.

For the first time in my life I did something wonderful, and took a carriage to the Strand, to Messrs. Coutts & Co. A crossing-sweeper dashed to open the carriage door, and I dropped a half penny into his hand, for all the world as if I were a rich lady.

And I was, for inside my bosom was a pouch with 20 gold coins in it.

Into the Bank I went, the doorman opening the door for me, the clerks rushing to greet me. The place held a smell of money and hypocrisy, dear Sophie, for they knew not who I was! And with the manager himself in attendance, I opened an account in the name of Clarisse Dayson. A new name, a new life! Just to mention the name of Alfred Lymardson brought a small sherry for me to drink, in a fine Waterford crystal glass, and such bowing and scraping as you would never see in a hundred years in our home! Ah, if only he knew! but I have found in the great City of London that what people do not know does not of any consequence hurt them. They go by appearances, and my appearance, in Serenia's dress so carefully altered to fit my own figure, stood the test of their eyes. They took me for a rich lady wanting an account. And so I am. For is not 20 gold coins a fortune to one who had nothing?

And Sophie dear, there will be no more. Much much more. Because -

Ah, let me for now keep those thoughts in my head! I may well return to them in time.

I made my move to deposit my money, dear sister, because I fear things are Not Well with dear Alfred and I do not wish to have money in the house for fear of him asking for it and me, being beholden to him as I am, would have to hand it over.

I have this feeling only, it is nothing like definite. But you see, more and more lately he has thrown tempers which have shaken this house to its foundations. Cook had bidden us all be silent when we are near him, Lizzy has been ordered to come only every other day, and Dominica now has to see to the boots and the yard. Briggs said at breakfast this very morning it does not bode well, that Mr Alfred leaves his friends' house with a face like thunder clouds and he afeared for his job. I don't fear for myself, for with my knowledge what men really want of me I can go and find someone else if I must. I would prefer though to stay here, for Alfred, when things go well, is the kindest of men.

You have always said luck is a fickle companion, and so it is. You said it once when the cheapjack came calling, remember that, sister? Remember when we gathered in the bright sunshine of an August day - was it only a year ago? - to watch the cheapjack lay out his goods upon the ground, and entertain the folk of the village with Chase the Lady, and you refused to take part. I do not know whether it was because Verger was close by and you feared his tongue a tattling to Father or whether you meant what you said but you refused to join in even without a coin to lay down for a bet.

"Luck is a fickle companion" you said in a loud voice and stood back, letting others bet their farthings and half pennies, and indeed lose.

I fear Alfred is losing these days. His actions are more devious and his intentions more - dastardly? Let me tell you.

Three nights ago Alfred entertained a whole crowd of people I had not seen before. These were men unlike those I had come across, these were men with hard faces and hard minds, for their talk was coarse when only I was present, and their tongues loosened with drink.

I made to leave on two occasions; each time Alfred detained me at the door, a gentle hand on my arm, a whisper of his spirit scented breath in my ear.

"Please stay, it is for my future" and each time I turned back from the door and went back to my place, on a footstool at Alfred's feet, for all the world as if I were his slave.

And indeed I am. Alfred may not have laid with me or toyed with me, never once had my breast felt the touch of his hand, my body felt the crush of his arms, my lips felt the heat of his mouth, yet for all that I am Alfred's slave for I owe him so much! Did he not rescue me from a fate worse than death the day he found me on the station platform afraid and alone? And did he not out of the goodness of his heart give me a home and a room of my own? And a position when I had none?

Ah, Sophie, I can see you now shaking your head over these words - were I to send them to you! and saying

"But dear Clarisse, you have given your body to those he knows, you have felt the sting of the strap and the pain of the slipper and the thrust of a man's manhood and all that, for what?"

For my pleasure. For ever it was my pleasure, for ever it was my desire to have such things. The money, the coins now safely in the bank under a name I shall not tell Alfred, came as an extra to my pleasure. My pleasure has paid for my future.

But this night it was very different, very different indeed.

After everyone had drunk heavily of the mead and ale decanters, so he called for quiet among the babble of voices and beckoned to me to stand. I did, and breathed in the heavy cigar smoke and body odour of the men, for they were sweating in the warm evening and had drunk and eaten well.

"My Clarisse here has a story to tell you. Clarisse, dear, tell these gentlemen of the thrashing your father and the elders gave you."

A coldness began to squeeze around my heart, for I began to have an inkling of why I had been detained, why Dominica had been sent away, why Cook was ordered to stay in her quarters and only I summoned to the evening of men.

I thought swiftly of the home I had and the secure position I had, and the money in the bank, and that made me smile. I stood up, and took my skirts in one hand, swaying slightly as I turned round and round, to face them all.

And I told them in great and gory detail of That Punishment Session, told how the strap fell over and over again.

And saw their faces go red and their breath come harsh and the hands squeeze tight around the tankards. I raised my skirts very slightly higher and saw the eyes, saw them turn downwards, saw them focus in on the feet and ankles, the feet in black leather slippers so fine and soft and the ankles so slim and elegant and turned for their pleasure. And then raised a little higher so they caught a glimpse of calf and white stocking.

And oh Sophie I knew what was to come and I went warm inside, as warm as the toast on the end of a fork held before a blazing fire. Alfred stood up and without a word fetched the bench from the hall where it normally stayed to hold Alfred's boots. It was clean, and I knew this had been long planned in Alfred's mind, and that Dominica or Lizzy had been told to clean it.

Without him asking I laid down over the bench and let one of the visitors, one of the esteemed guests, who probably held credit notes from Alfred, remove my clothes. And I let another tie my wrists and ankles to the bench legs with thin strips of leather that gave slightly and I could have escaped had I wanted to, but he was not to know that, for the look of satisfaction he gave me when he stood back told me so.

Alfred produced a leather belt, one I had seen him wear in the past, and which I knew then to be soft and flexible and I closed my eyes tight as the first man approached me.

I thought Cornelius was a hard man, Sophie, but these men were hard. These men knew how to use a belt with maximum strength and maximum pain and every single one burned me through and I could not help but shout and scream and that excited them more. With harsh words and exhortations to each other to

"Make the whore sing louder!" each man in turn gave me ten strokes, and would have done more had Alfred permitted it.

Sophie, my dear sister, there were eight of them.

How I cried afterwards, when the belt stung so much and hurt so much and my hips felt on fire where they had lashed me and drawn blood with the tip and I felt crushed against the hardness of the bench and it was like Papa's thrashing all over again. Then they drew lots to see who would have me and the biggest man among them whooped with delight when he had the result of the draw.

I was untied and again without being told took the man by the hand and led him to the dining room which was empty and quiet and where no eyes could watch us.

And there I disrobed for him while he watched and I took him into my body with all the lust I had, which was plenty after such a thrashing which left my body singing with emotion.

Big he was everywhere but there, a small man there, small enough to fit into my hand.

"How did you know?" he asked as he pushed and pushed against me and made no impression but I would not for the world let him know! "How did you know I wished to be alone with you so no one could see?" and I knew he knew I knew his shameful secret. But he came mightily into me and was well pleased, and gave me a half sovereign which I was exhorted not to show Alfred, and I stowed it in my bosom in a reticule I now keep there for that purpose.

We adjusted our clothes, I dressed again fast and we went back to join the others. I once again sat at Alfred's feet, for all that it hurt so much to sit! and the men stared at me with hungry eyes.

"How much for a night?" one man asked, and Alfred shook his head.

"Clarisse sleeps here and nowhere else. She has no need of night-time company."

Maybe that is true but sometimes I do long for daytime friends.

My sister, how I miss you! For all that London is a big city with people and excitement, with carriages and elegant ladies, men who are handsome and well dressed and well set up for life, I miss the smell of the honeysuckle and the call of the plover, I miss the sound of the night owl and the nightingale across our fields. The bark of a dog reminds me of a dog fox prowling, and I fear of the chickens in theirhouse. I long for the sound of a bed as someone moves in their sleep, the sighs of those who are dreaming, the clump of Papa's footsteps as he checks the house when he cannot sleep. Afeared of robbers as always. Does Papa still do that, Sophie? Does he still walk the corridors at night and the sound of his feet in passing are so like the sound of the watch here to tell me 'all's well'.

All's well.

I ache from 80 blows with a belt, I ache from the merciless thrusting of a man with a small handle desperate to get more reaction from me - for all that I acted and twisted and cried out in mock passion.

I ache for a man.

Alfred is a fine man, Sophie, a fine man, but I long for a Master, someone who can truly and completely and overwhelmingly make me his slave.

If he is out there, I pray I find him before it is too late, before I am so ill used no man will look at me.

Is this me, the Clarisse who so boldly said all future lovers would not be men?

Perhaps it is because Serenia has not called for a few days, because the men here are stronger and firmer and longer lasting than her tinkling fingers - or is it just that I am made to be slave to a man?

For whatever reason, I ache.

But I have another half sovereign to put away, to add to the fast growing fortune, and that is not something to be scorned.

If I have enough money I can buy what I want.

Is that not true?

CHAPTER 8
IT WAS UNREAL.

Each day Lauren got up early, boiled kettles, washed herself carefully, chose only her prettiest undies - the dustbin overflowing with ordinary plain cotton knickers no longer considered suitable for work. And each day she drove to the station in a state of high tension, coped with words that ran all over the pages of her book while the train rushed her to London and destiny -

Which didn't happen.

Each day Lauren was at her desk by 9.30, machine switched on and humming, ready for the day. Often her earphones would be in and she would be typing before the others had thrown open the door, breezed in with their 'good morning' and bags thrown down, cold drinks put on the desk, sighs at having to work in an office while the sun shone outside.

"You're keen," observed Stella one morning, when for the third day in a row she had come in to find Lauren at her desk and working.

Lauren smiled at her over the typewriter.

"It's that or work late, there's so much to do at the moment." And they bought her story. After all, they had seen her stay late - just the once.

Each day Judith came in at her usual 10 am. Lauren would immediately jump up, make a black coffee and take it in to her boss, who would glance at her as if she was no more than the junior.

"Thanks, Lauren," and she would get down to the pile of post which always seemed to materialise on her blotter. Lauren began to believe the whole conversation had been a dream, a figment of her over-ripe imagination. This cool person, this efficient boss with her analytical mind and immediate grasp of all salient facts, could not be the person who sat by her desk, sweaty palmed and hopeful, that hot night.

But at home hidden under a pile of lacy briefs, was a book which proved otherwise. A book which came in a brown paper bag which shouted 'private' even as you looked at it. A book which told of delights in store for those who had bottoms willing to take pain. For beneath the pain lies pleasure such as few will know, for few will take the dangerous step forward to asking for that pain.

And then something else happened to prove to Lauren it wasn't all a figment of her imagination. One morning, as she coped with a huge pile of filing which had somehow appeared, she left the top drawer open when she opened the second one and the entire cabinet began to tilt. In a panic Lauren slammed her hand to the back of the cabinet.

And found a hook.

Hanging from it was a cane.

She pushed the cabinet back, closed both drawers and stood holding the filing, her hands shaking, her knees trembling so much it was all she could do to stand up.

She did mean it. It will happen again. It's just that it has to happen in her own good time, at her command, not when I want it to.

On a sudden impulse Lauren walked swiftly round Judith's desk and opened the middle drawer. Under a pile of blotting paper she found a three tailed tawse, flexible and lethal.

She closed the drawer sharply, afraid of being caught spying and prying, afraid of what else she might find. That was enough to be going on with!

Hearing voices outside, hearing footsteps along the corridor, Lauren went back to the filing with renewed determination. By the time she heard Judith's distinctive voice in the outer office it was almost done.

Judith flung open the door and walked in, smiling at Lauren.

"Oh good, I was going to mention the filing. Thanks."

"I'll get your coffee." Lauren ducked out of the way, back out into the office and got the kettle going. Stella smirked at her over the photocopying machine.

"Little slave, aren't you? Make Judith's coffee as soon as she comes in!"

Lauren ignored her. Stella had come out with the odd jibe before, when Lauren appeared to be doing too much for her boss. Stella, she noticed, did as little as possible. Mr Hazelton hadn't made a wise move when he took her on. On the other hand, if he hadn't, she, Lauren, would be working for him instead and she would never have had this relationship with Judith.

While she returned to the office with the coffee, Judith glanced up at her.

"Ignore the silly bitch," she said in a low voice only Lauren could have heard. "She's jealous of your ability to do things which please me, that's all." Her hand went to her ears and she looked up in shock.

"Forget my earrings! Oh, I feel as if I've come out without knickers on."

"But you always take them off when you get here," Lauren protested mildly, amused by the reaction. Every day Judith came in she would remove her clip on earrings and leave them by the telephone as a matter of course. Judith stared at her, and a new look crept into her eyes.

"Criticism? All right, Lauren Sanderson, you can go out lunch time and buy a hairbrush, one with a flat wide back. I don't care where you get it from, just get it and bring it. And be prepared to stay late."

Melting again, wetness flooding her lacy briefs, Lauren said nothing, just nodded and left the office. Had Judith been waiting for an opportunity, or to get her nerve together to issue an order? Had the right moment been so long in coming? Whatever, it had happened, it was here.

Where could she buy a hairbrush? Chemists, try the local chemists, or the hairdressing salon down the road from the office, or the branch of Woolworths in the Strand, that would do, but it meant a hard slog to get there in the lunch hour and back - but an order was an order.

"Boss pleased with her coffee?" enquired Stella sweetly.

Lauren smiled. "Certainly is, Stella, certainly is. Is Mr Hazelton pleased with the amount of work you get done?" She slipped her earphones in before Stella could answer her.

Lunchtime found Lauren hurrying for the stairs, all three flights down to the busy hustling street outside. Hairbrush. It had been hard not to type the word over and over again in memos and letters, it was so up front of her mind!

The hairdressing salon smelled of perm lotion, of hair spray and shampoo. The assistant came over as Lauren pushed her way through the potted palms and stands of hair accessories to the desk.

"I'm after a good quality hairbrush, you know, nice wide back, strong bristles." The words came rolling out as if she had planned them. In fact, her tongue was all but glued to the roof of her mouth.

"Have a look over there." The girl indicated another revolving stand of brushes. With relief Lauren realised her request wasn't going to be noted and commented on, she was just another customer. It's all in my mind, blowing this up all out of proportion, she thought, as she spun the metal round, checking the brushes, looking for one that would please Judith.

She went back to the desk with a wooden backed brush, the cost making her wince. Well it was worth it to obey an order. Her very first, her very first test of obedience.

"This looks like a good one," she told the girl.

"This is good, you picked one of the best ones." The girl wrapped the brush, took the money and the till jangled as she rattled change. "Here you are. Nice hair you've got, if ever you want to be a model, come in - the boss would be pleased to dress hair like that."

"Thanks, I'll remember that," Lauren promised, dismissing the thought the moment she got outside. The temptation to unwrap the brush, to stare at it, was overwhelming, but she had to wait. Instead she queued for a cheese sandwich and fresh green apple in the local sandwich bar, where the owner knew her and winked over the counter.

"How's my redhead today? You got some twinkle in your eyes, what did you do last night?" he jested as he wrapped her order.

"Nothing much." But she had, last night Lauren had read the book again, lying flat on her back, vibrator tickling the inside of the circle of muscle that contracted sharply with every flash of passion that ran through her.

"In that case you're thinking about tonight." Lauren blushed. He was closer than she wanted him to be. He laughed, waved and said "Enjoy yourself!" as he turned to the next customer.

The afternoon was interminable. Lauren wriggled on her seat, glad she was in the corner where only Linda could see her if she turned away from the switchboard.

Fortunately for Lauren the afternoon calls kept Linda busy and then there was the post to deal with, so she didn't see Lauren's twitchings and movements. Lauren dropped the wrapped hairbrush on the desk when she collected some of the post.

"I'll leave at 5.30 and come back, all right?"

Judith nodded and went on signing letters.

"Going home tonight for a change?" Liz smiled. Lauren knew there was no malice behind her words, it was only Stella she had to watch out for.

"Yes, thought I'd go home." They all clattered down the stairs together, talking of that night's TV, of things they were going to do. Lauren turned right, the other two turned left and walked off along the road. Lauren stopped at the restaurant two doors away from the office, watched until Liz and Stella were out of sight and then slowly and calmly walked back in the door and up the stairs to the office.

Mike Hazelton was half way down the stairs.

"Lauren, forgotten something?"

"Yes, I won't be a moment."

"It's all right Judith's still there, you can get in. Good night."

I KNOW JUDITH'S THERE! "Good night, see you tomorrow."

Lauren ran up the last flight, her heart pounding wildly. The door opened easily, once again the feeling of coming home swept over her, and she slipped, cautious as a cat burglar, into her own work place. Crazy.

Judith opened her office door and beckoned to her. Lauren took a deep breath and walked in.

"Just give me fifteen minutes to make sure everyone's gone and I'll go and lock the door. You can spend that fifteen minutes standing there, knickers round your knees please! and think about what I'm going to do."

The hairbrush lay in the middle of the blotter, new, clean, unmarked. The wrapper was nowhere to be seen, obviously Judith had disposed of it. She went on casually reading a file as if it were the most normal thing in the world that Lauren should stand by the filing cabinet, the one hiding the guilty secret she had discovered, and wait, nerves fluttering madly, briefs fluttering madly, colour pulsing and receding from her face.

Judith glanced at her watch, got up and walked to the door.

"Bend over the desk. I'll spank you when I come back." She walked out, leaving Lauren alone with her thoughts.

Now was her chance - no, no backing out now! She had stayed late, she had bought the hairbrush as ordered, she had given up her job as ordered - against Ray's protests - and this was pay off time.

The outer door was firmly locked, Lauren heard Judith rattle the handle to be sure. There was a long pause. Lauren leaned over the desk, face cushioned on her crossed arms, legs straight and firm, waiting, stomach churning with apprehension, fear a dull taste in her mouth, desire a strong throbbing emotion between her legs.

Judith came back eventually. Lauren lay still, a sinking feeling engulfing her. Now? Was it to be now?

"Good. I just checked all the offices to make sure no one was there, no one can hear anything. Now - "

She walked round her desk and pushed her chair back.

"I've changed my mind, come over here."

Lauren walked round the desk, stood by Judith's side, saw the look of clear anticipation and pleasure and laid down across Judith's firm thighs without being asked. Her skirt was turned back, a warm hand slid over her cheeks, separated them, touched them with a lover's caress. Then there was nothing but coolness, nothing but a rustling sound as the hair brush left the desk.

"This is going to hurt" - and the brush came down square in the middle of one cheek.

It did hurt, a sudden flare of pain as the brush hit the other cheek, equally hard. Lauren yelped and involuntarily squirmed.

"Be still." Judith held Lauren firmly, a hand in the middle of her back. "Hands out of the way!" The brush came down again and again, and then Judith settled into a rhythm of steady spanks, hard, covering each inch of skin firmly, the brush leaving pain behind that really shuddered through Lauren. This is it, she told herself, lying face down, the brush finding her with equal severity every single time. Tears sprang to her eyes and she began to feel terribly uncomfortable, and humiliated at being put in the position of a child, being spanked like that. The carpet looked worn, the smell of dust and history came to her as she tried to be still, tried not to offend by wriggling but it hurt!

This is what you've always visualised! she told herself, feeling even more foolish as the spanking went on, more painful than she ever dreamed, more humiliating than she ever appreciated, more exciting than she had ever read.

Judith stopped, pushed Lauren to her feet, looked at the bright red face and unshed tears and smiled.

"For a first time I was pretty hard, wasn't I?" Lauren nodded, afraid to commit herself to speech. It hurt terribly, she could do nothing but clutch the burning cheeks, try and rub away some of the pain, while all she was doing was increasing the feeling.

"I meant it to be." Judith leaned back in the chair, put the brush in her drawer, and reached for her handbag.

"I meant to be, because there can be no half measures. Next time I might spank you by hand, for the pleasure of feeling my hand on your skin. But - we have to make a start somewhere, and I wanted you to know I intend to be firm and severe with you. Is that understood?"

Lauren nodded again and eased her knickers back up. Judith watched her.

"And in future you'll not do that until I tell you, all right? How do you know I don't want to look at what I've done?"

"Sorry." Lauren held her skirt up. "Do you?"

"Not this time. Here's the money for the brush. You spent a lot, but you bought a good one. You were prepared to go short to obey the order. I like that, a lot. I also like the fact you're not crying."

"It hurts," Lauren admitted, clenching her teeth as she gratefully moved to pick up the money, the burning pain surging through her.

"It's meant to. Corporal punishment isn't any good unless it's really started hard - I have the option of going easy next time if I want to ... I'll unlock the door, you'll be wanting to go home."

Lauren coaxed a smile. "Do I say thank you or something?"

"Do you? That's for you to decide. As are future activities after a spanking, bring a vibrator to work if you want, we can have a lot of fun with that. It's up to you. I won't push that side of it. I'll just give you the punishments."

Out in the main office, Judith paused, the key turned in the lock. "By the way - "

Lauren looked at her, waiting for another revelation. The tone told her there was something to be said.

"That was my first time too. Good night Lauren, I'll see you in the morning."

"Good night - Mistress."

She slipped quietly out the door and began to walk slowly down the stairs, feeling the burning settle to the glow everyone talked about, the glow which reached her pubis, set it on fire.

Lauren paused on the stairs, not thinking, just feeling. Then, taking courage in both hands, she made a move bigger than the one which led her into Judith's office in the first place, she turned and went back up.

Judith was still waiting by the door.

CHAPTER 9
OCTOBER 1869

My dear Sister,

Last time I said you would be so proud of me, I wonder now what you would make of my newest experience?

Remember - ah sister, remember! sunlit days and dappled shade, the call of birds, the bright crunch of wheels on gravel as someone came to visit the house for tea and consolation! I wondered many times since what confidences Papa holds in his breast and whether they stir him as a man! Remember the thrill of trying to creep close to Papa's study to find out what people came for -

But memories are in another direction. This time I want to remember and for you to remember our riding days. Jacky was no great horse, no high stepping tail flourishing proud stallion, just a faithful and dogged pony. But how we love to pretend to be ladies riding around our field! Remember the feeling, dear Sophie, and most of all, remember the time Jacky got tired and stopped, throwing me over his head and landing me, skirts aflounder, on the grass?

Of all moments for Papa to come by, that was the moment. Summonsed to the study and berated for 'unseemly behaviour' and bent over Papa's horrid large desk for the sting of the switch across barely covered cheeks - oh how he did switch me that day! I remember still, with a twitch of my posterior, how I howled and cried and he beat me until I could not sit astride Jacky for three days!

Enough. What I have not told you so far is I have just found out, by accident, well - no.

I have just found out by eavesdropping that Serenia and Cornelius are brother and sister! I truthfully never considered their relationship! But there they are, living together in the house left by their parents, surrounded by servants and staff, sharing the same desires - and the money with which to do it! Some people are so lucky!

I have learned to submit to Cornelius without question.

"My good little maid" he called me one night, when I rose and stood naked before him, arms above my head, presenting every inch of skin to his plaited dressage whip, a savage instrument that cuts like nothing else. For sure my heart does leap within its cage when the whip appears in his hands, for all that I could cry and cry after the lash has found me!

I have also learned that submitting to Cornelius brings rewards.

This night Serenia came with him, carrying a soft green velvet riding suit in her arms, complete with feathered bonnet and high buttoned boots of pure soft brown leather!

"You ride, do you not? asked Serenia as she dressed me, as I turned and pirouetted before my triple glass which, fly stained though it be, showed me a touch of elegance that would be hard to describe, Sophie dear. For sure you have never seen me in such clothes!

"I rode at home" I answered, afraid to say it were nothing more than a sway-backed old pony whose idea of galloping was to move into a reluctant trot.

"Good!" She clapped her fair hands together, hands which I know from experience have power in them to sting, to raise red weals, to hurt and to punish! and cried

"Tomorrow, we must go riding tomorrow, Cornelius!" and he smiled his dark slow smile that turns my blood to water and my bowels to jelly - for all that he does stir me, I am afraid of this man.

"Of course, we must ask Alfred if he will release the fair maid for a ride in the afternoon. And you will wear the outfit." He turned to me, so dark, so strong so sure of himself! "Alfred has no horses of his own but I can provide a mount for you from my stable. And afterwards, you can come and eat with us."

"But - "

˗ "But what, dear Clarisse?" Serenia, arms around me, lips too close to mind for comfort and peace of mind.

"I am but a servant, I cannot eat with you!" and the voice whispered it so low Serenia would never have heard had she not been that close. She kissed me full on the lips and held me to her body, pulling my loins close to hers.

"Clarisse, never think of yourself as a servant. You are a woman in your own right, you have womanly desires and needs, you obey Cornelius as a good maid should, not as a servant does, for not once have you ever called him Sir." And she was right, Sophie, I never had! For all the times he had come to me, for all the thrashings I had received at his hands, for all the occasions when he had berated me for not obeying an order as fast as he would like, and do I not do it so he can have further excuse to beat me and beat me hard? I have not bowed to him as a Master and I as a servant.

And he spoke, in a serious and firm voice.

"I come to you because you have never called me Sir, because your will is not broken, because you give yourself to me from desire and not from a sense of duty or terms of employment. I like a woman with spirit and fire, Clarisse, and you have all those things. In fact, I am thinking of asking Alfred to let you go, to come and live with us."

And with that, dear sister, my heart was fit to catch short in my throat! Live with Serenia and Cornelius, to be treated as a family member, to be -

But Alfred has been so good to me! Alfred has given me home and shelter, and this was my home this -

"This you call home?" Did Cornelius read my thoughts, I wonder? "This beggarly room? Come with us, Clarisse, and experience the real luxury of living, for you shall have an honoured place in our house."

"And you'll be there for us all the time, and we will love one another, all three of us!" Serenia was excited, I could see that, her eyes flashed and her breath was coming short and hard.

I stood in my green velvet riding suit and thought of Alfred losing to his many friends, and wondering how I would live if it all fell apart, as it might.

"Poor dear, you have confused and confounded her!" Serenia laughed. "Come now, put that suit away, Clarisse, and come here, for I have a desire to strap you hard tonight."

I took off the suit, dear sister, and I went across Serenia's knees and was strapped hard, while Cornelius stood and urged her on with words such as

"Harder!" and

"Here! The thighs are white!" and I wriggled and writhed and struggled and fought the strap for all that I longed for the sting just the second before it landed on me. And after I lay on my bed with Cornelius at back of me, thrusting hard into that which his sister had just punished and his sister herself with fingers and lips at my breasts and secret place and I came and came and came in waves of sheer pleasure which few are given to experience.

"Tomorrow, at 3, we will go riding," Serenia promised as they took their leave, as I lay exhausted and weary but glowing with feeling and loving the green velvet riding suit which hung from the hook.

Riding!

And yes, dear sister, we did go riding. Such a glorious afternoon! October sunshine, pale washed blue sky, golden leaves falling, crunching under the horses's hooves, touch of chill in the air, enough to make me proud and glad I was wearing green velvet, for it touched and fitted me well, and kept me warm.

I looked a little foolish, I warrant, not being sure of myself sitting so high from the ground on the back of a magnificent chestnut gelding that pranced its way along the bridle paths in the Royal Park. Serenia put it down to the fact I was riding side saddle for the first time.

"How sweet she looks, Cornelius!" she said, and perhaps I did. I felt nervous, dear Sophie, wondering if I would fall and make myself look a fool, if not damage myself quite considerably!

Serenia rode a black horse, and Cornelius a brown stallion, animals which they called by name, and the horses pricked up their ears and responded with scarcely a touch of the heels. When Cornelius took off at a gallop and Serenia followed, it was all I could do to remain where I was, plodding delicately along, holding the reins in my right hand, clutching the saddle with my left, scared stiff and scared to show it! Serenia wheeled her horse and galloped back to me, pulling up short and smiling.

"So sorry, my dear Clarisse, we didn't mean to leave you! Juniper will gallop if you wish!"

"No thank you, let me enjoy the afternoon quietly, it has been a long time since I rode." They rode off again wildly, pounding across the green together, such a handsome couple it was hard to believe they were not married! a look a touch they understood one another perfectly, these new people who had come into my life with violence, with pain, with new experience, and now with an offer of a home.

For it was still in my mind they had asked me to go and live with them, for all it was phrased differently. I knew I could refuse, could say I wished to stay with Alfred and they would have to agree.

But did I?

As the afternoon glowed its golden October sunshine, trees glowed their golden Autumn colours, my thoughts turned from Alfred's glowing kindness to the golden feelings of passion aroused by Serenia and Cornelius, so I knew I would go. For nothing is more golden than security and Alfred did not offer me security any longer.

I did of course pay for my afternoon's pleasure of riding, and what pleasure it was! Once I had control of my horse and realised it would do what I wanted, not what it wanted, not like dear Jacky! I rode at a trot around the paths, saw the people step back, men doffed their hats to me, women smiled, children waved and called out, and it felt good.

I paid when we got back to the stables, when Cornelius helped me dismount, and immediately caught my wrists together, tied them with the halter rein and tied that in turn to a manger. Then, with Serenia holding up my skirts and with Serenia's fingers deep in a wet slit brought about by knowing what they were likely to do, I stood and took the riding crop across my cheeks, my thighs, and then turned for the front of my thighs to be punished too. And then Serenia pushed me back and loved me.

And I whispered I would live with them forever.

So, dear sister, I shall be packing up my belongings after I close this letter to you, and begin to the move to my new home.

Alfred was upset, but not as much as I had feared, for he must have seen the move coming, must have heard some whisper of their intentions from his friends. And, I admit it now, there was a flicker of relief too. For the losing was going on and on, and Alfred had fears of his own.

I have just one problem.

Briggs is going too. To the new home.

I hate and fear that man.

But it is possible it is very possible I can but hope! Serenia will keep him in the stables, where he belongs!

In time all will be revealed, dear Sophie, in the letters I dare not send.

CHAPTER 10
OCTOBER 1969

Lauren again counted the money stored in the back of her purse, marvelling at the fact she had managed to save £50 in a few weeks. £50! Up to now every penny had gone on petrol, the rent for the dingy caravan, and fares to work. Eating had come a poor fourth in the equation, sometimes she skipped lunch altogether, settling for a cheap snack from the local sandwich bar. Now it was different, now everything was different.

Judith paid for lunch, discreetly, money slid over the desk when no one was around, and not a word passing between them. She had also slipped a £50 note in an envelope marked 'memo' and left it under the typewriter cover for Lauren to find. That had paid the fares for a long time.

Lauren said nothing to anyone, some things were best kept to herself, but one lunch time she hastily brushed out her dark red hair, straightened her blouse and skirt, slipped on a suit jacket and made her way with some boldness but a lot of inner trembling to Coutts & Co. to open a savings account for herself. Everyone was so polite, she mused, as she walked out, her new account number safely stored in her bag, and a new confidence in herself putting a glow on her face. Several men paused to look at her as she walked by, their attention flattering her even more.

It was almost worth celebrating with a drink in a wine bar, but she hesitated on the doorstep, blocked by a barrage of wine smells and loud voices, of stares and critical comments and turned away, settling instead for the restaurant and the funny Italian waiter who knew her even from her infrequent visits. He found her a small table, put Reserved on the other side so she wouldn't be bothered, and handed her a menu, all done with a smile and pure Italian courtesy and warmth. Lauren smiled to herself. This was how it should be all the time, and this was how it was going to be.

Savings. For the first time in a very long time, money tucked away, and she was determined to leave it there.

Hard come by, her savings, paid for with tears, for Judith had reduced her to tears, with smiles, when they laughed afterwards over her striped bottom and trembling knees, over the fact they loved one another so deeply it was like a kind of telepathy. Each day Lauren dressed with care, not knowing if she would be asked to stay, not knowing how she would be treated. Each day was an adventure in itself, with Judith sometimes friendly and warm, sometimes even loving, but other times cold and hard, issuing orders in a commanding voice. It was those days Lauren ran to obey. But all her obedience, all her piles of neatly typed letters and prepared papers, didn't avoid the command 'stay late', sometimes dictated along with the letters, sometimes whispered over the desk at the end of the day.

When everyone had left, Stella with spiteful comments about 'sucking up to the boss again for a rise' when everyone knew wages were being kept down, Lauren would sit at her desk, fingers poised over the keys, pretending to be busy while her heart pounded hard in her chest and her body quivered in anticipation.

Only when the offices were completely empty and the door locked would Judith come back to her, stand in front of her desk and begin the orders.

The first time was the hairbrush spanking, a long drawn out affair that left Lauren scared and shaking, but longing for more - when she got home and thought about it.

The second occasion had been as Judith had requested, a hand spanking, softness and hardness, the firm square hand descending again and again, curving to fit the cheeks it spanked, a sensation unlike anything Lauren had ever dreamed it would be. When Judith was tired, or her hand hurt (she never admitted to either but one had to be the case) she picked up a ruler and dealt twelve fast blows to the reddened cheeks, making Lauren gasp in pain and astonishment.

The chair on which Lauren sat had been used several times. A typist's chair swivels alarmingly easily, and Judith made full use of that fact. She had ordered Lauren to kneel on it, knowing that every blow of the tawse would send her moving, and would not bring the chair back, but lashed out again and again, catching Lauren's thighs and hips, her back at times, her bottom always, wide bands of red that sent her into paroxysm of agony. It hurt far more than she had ever considered, ever could visualise, but it was also more exciting than she ever dreamed, the anticipation building to a point when work became almost impossible, and she would have to go and sit quietly somewhere for a little while to reduce her feelings to a level where it was not so obvious.

"Listen carefully." Judith's voice whispering in her ears through the earphones. Lauren paused, a file half opened, expectant, awaiting an order of some kind. "Mr Williams has told me there's a flat going upstairs, above these offices. Are you interested? I'll help you pay the rent. I'm sure you don't want to stay in that scrubby caravan of yours much longer. Think about it. You could sell your car and save on fares too."

"Damn, it's raining." Linda reached for her coat. "I have to get some stamps too." Lauren looked out of the window, saw the rain beginning to fall a little harder, and then stood up.

"Judith's gone to Court without her coat, I'll take it over to her."

"Good little slave, aren't you?" sniggered Stella. Lauren ignored her, fetched Judith's coat from her office and hurried our of the door.

The Law Courts were crowded as usual, bewigged and gowned barristers rushing around with their arms full of papers and books, their pupils hurrying along behind them with even more books. Here and there a man stood ramrod straight and tall, ex Army or police turned private detective. You could pick them out every time. It was as if they were stamped out of a mould, mused Lauren, hurrying past them to the Divorce Courts.

Judith was deep in conversation with a tall barrister. Black curls peeked from beneath the grey wig as he leaned closer.

"Lauren! What a surprise!" Judith smiled at her, took in the damp shoulders and hair, and her own coat over Lauren's arm, and her smile grew bigger. "Thank you, dear."

"Your own personal slave?" asked the barrister.

Judith turned to him. "Roger Grant, this is Lauren Sanderson, my secretary and slave. Lauren, this is Roger Grant."

He bowed to her, and smiled.

"I wish I had a personal slave like you, how thoughtful you are!"

Lauren ducked her head, flushed but said nothing. Judith laughed.

"I'm getting her well trained, Roger, as you can see!"

"I'd like to borrow her occasionally." The words were said seriously. Judith stiffened, her eyes flashed with interest and she took Lauren's hand.

"We'd like that, wouldn't we?"

"Yes, Judith." And indeed Lauren's heart fluttered twice as fast as the thought of being sent or handed over or whatever to this good looking man. She wondered how the conversation had changed so fast, how the situation had changed so fast, with so few words being spoken.

Roger stood up straight, shook his gown around his shoulders and moved away slightly.

"Call me at Chambers. We'll arrange something, soon,"

"Will do."

He strode away through the crowds, shouting a greeting to another barrister, a solicitor, acknowledged the salute of another, and was gone.

Judith turned to Lauren, her eyes gleaming.

"Now there's something new! We'll explore that, you and I. You'll like being sent to someone else, won't you?" There was no need for an answer. Together they set off towards the exit, both deep in thought.

Before they reached the street Lauren paused, a hand on Judith's arm.

"I'd like to see the flat, if I may," she said carefully, unaware that she had even reached a decision.

Judith nodded. "Mr Williams said just to ask for the key, I'll do that for you. You can go up later, after work if you like."

"It would save me a lot of money."

"Of course, and it would be far more convenient for us too, wouldn't it?" That of course was the second thought which had crowded in on the heels of the first.

And that was the real reason she had asked about the flat.

Mr Williams, small thin and taking his caretaker's job very seriously, showed them the flat, and then left them alone. Two rooms, kitchen and bathroom, it was palatial after the poky scruffy caravan she called home. Judith walked across the thick rug to the window and looked down.

"You can see right into Fleet Street from here." Lauren walked over to join her, saw how the view took her across London rooftops, saw the bustle and chaos of Fleet Street below her, but heard only the muted sound of traffic and people. She looked around the room again. It was large, with soaring high ceiling and a sense of space and light. A hint of perfume seemed to linger, a scent of flowers long gone, a musky smell that spoke of love and passion, of happiness and friendship. Lauren shook her head. I'm being very foolish now! It's just the change after my caravan, that's all.

The bedroom was equally as large, with huge built in wardrobes and a window seat. The kitchen, small but well fitted out, and the bathroom - even to have a bathroom was pleasure enough right now! Lauren thought of all the hasty wash downs, the walk in darkness to the outside loo, and breathed a huge sigh of relief.

"Please?" She turned to Judith, pleading with every part of her, she wanted the flat. "I'll need some furniture," she went on, speaking as if she had reservations, but her heart was beating madly with pleasure. This could be mine! I'd sleep on the floor rather than go back to that hole!

"Of course. We'll arrange it. It'll be in my name, so no one need know. You can go and give notice on your home, sell the car after you move your bits and pieces here, and we'll see about the rest. We can pick up some furniture for you."

Yes, thought Lauren, second hand, comfortable, already looking as if it had been used and loved, that's what this place needs. It doesn't want new bright shiny furniture. It wants love.

And wondered why she should think that.

Judith's arms went around her.

"You can have the cane for the first time the day you move in."

A flood of emotions went through Lauren, dampening her knickers, bringing a flush of colour to her face that made Judith smile.

"And - " Judith added, turning away and walking toward the door. "I phoned Roger Grant. You go and visit him next Wednesday. 7 pm sharp. He says he will be waiting for you. You're to go alone this time, and be sure I'LL be waiting for you when you get back.

CHAPTER 11
MY DEAR SISTER,

I am writing to you from my new home.

Alfred did cry a tear or two when I left, Sophie, believe it or not. Cook held me close, said she hoped I knew what it was I wanted and would get it from life safely, for I was too good a person to allow myself to be swept away on a tide of evil doing. I know she meant Cornelius and Serenia, but I said nothing, just hugged her back, for the homely lady had been good to me. And Alfred, how I held him close! How I cried on his velvet shoulder before Serenia tugged at my arm, telling me the hansom cab was waiting for me! I snatched up my small reticule and bag of belongings and was gone without a backward glance. If I had looked back, all would have been lost.

But I do confess to this letter, Sophie, that Alfred had told me if I had not asked to leave, I would have had to go anyway for the loses were mounting and soon the home would go if Luck did not change for him. His tears were as much for the possible future as for my leaving. I knew it, but for all that, I was sore hurt in my heart.

Serenia chattered on as the cab wound its way through the streets, past flower sellers and policemen, past road sweepers and cabs awaiting a fare, past newspaper sellers and beggars. She chattered of inconsequential things, of Cornelius and his likes and dislikes, of their other home in Richmond, of how I would relieve them of the burden of keeping servants here in London when they were not often there, and I began to see how useful I would be. That lifted my sadness at leaving Alfred, and I felt a great sweep of joy go through me, and I looked - nay stared - out of the hansom cab at the sights we passed.

Oh how elegant London is! Fine gas lamps stand sentinel on the pavements, fine buildings with graceful trees graced the streets, the ladies with their huge hats and smiling faces, gentlemen in top hats and boys in flat caps, so much colour everywhere for all that it is late in the year! How golden the leaves which drifted down, how bright and cold the sky above me!

And we arrived and alighted in Fleet Street, which is where Serenia and Cornelius live when they are in London. We entered this quiet subdued yet elegant building, climbed the curved wooden stairs, and entered one of the many doors - and into my new home.

My home, oh Sophie, my home! I am at the top of this fine building, I have a large room with huge windows which look down on this bustling street, a large bedroom with a wardrobe, somewhere to hang my clothes! There is a small room for my own bath, and another small room where I can put my table and chair and where I will continue to write my letters. I do feel it is unseemly to sit in my lounge and write! Oh such luxury! Oh such rooms! Serenia has furnished my rooms with her own fair hand, Sophie! Brought me a couch and table, a lamp and hangings for the large windows, a bed on which -

A bed on which we will be together when it suits her to come to me.

For I am aware there is a price for all this luxury and it may be a high one.

I go down a flight of stairs which curve to fit the building, and into the quarters which belong to Serenia. These are beyond description, my dear sister, hangings such as you have never seen, rich velvet drapes held with heavy gold cord frame the windows, a richness of rugs on the floor, gold framed mirrors and huge portraits, elaborate furniture with thick tapestry upholstery, oak table and sideboard, silver and glass abound. This is for me to clean and care for, when Serenia is in Richmond. Oh, what can the other home be like, if this is only the London home? There is a small room by the side where Serenia's personal maid stays, so she says.

Go down another flight of stairs into the rooms which are occupied by Cornelius. Here it is manly, with leather and wood, a huge globe stands in one corner, here there are no portraits but sailing ships and maps, here decanters of fine-cut glass and a table at which he sits with his maps around him. This is very much a man's room. And of course a room for his valet.

And the floor below is where they entertain. Yes, dear Sister, they do not entertain in their own rooms! They have this huge room where there are velvet covered love seats and couches where the mirrors are enormous and lit by gas mantles which glow so secretly and goldenly in the evenings! Here the floor is covered with one huge Persian rug which can be rolled up if there is dancing or a party, here there are huge cupboards and sideboard laden with silver salvers and dish covers.

"This is not your worry!" Serenia told me, her arm around my waist. "This is where we entertain so this is where the hired staff come. There is a small room out there for the servants who are hired for the night."

It is from here, from beyond this large room that the kitchen and laundry rooms are situated. Such rooms you have never seen! A larder large enough to live in holds marble shelving, and racks for the meat, the vegetables, the pans, with utensils, with hanging racks for herbs and all other things. I was so amazed I stood with my mouth dropped open and Serenia closed it for me, saying I would catch flies better than the arsenic soaked flypaper hanging from the ceiling should I be stood like that much longer!

"When we are here we will bring our Cook with us." She smiled, seeing my amazement turn to apprehension in a moment as I realised what might be asked of me. I am not a cook! "But when we are not here, it is for you to cook your own meals, my dear Clarisse, and do not I beg you go short of food, for Cornelius likes your plumpness and will be sore offended if you should become thin like beggar women outside" and at that my heart did sink like a stone in the Thames, for was I not just thinking I could give the beggar women something from my table!

"They do not deserve that we can give" she went on and I was afeared in my heart she knew my thoughts. "And should you give just once, they will be on the stairs and give the house a bad name." And so I vowed to give money to the beggars far from here so that my friends would not be offended.

A home full of such money and luxury as you would never believe in your wildest dreams. And thanks to great luck and divine intervention I am part of it!

The house is empty tonight. Serenia and Cornelius have left for Richmond, taking the man Briggs with them, for he too has come from Alfred to work for them, but he will be at Richmond, so Serenia said. I am glad, for I am afeared of that man, and know not why.

I am here alone. And now I can set down that which has excited and troubled me since the moment I found it.

There is a small room here which no one has pointed out to me but which I found while wandering around with duster and beeswax looking for something to polish. No, I had no right to be there, my duster and polish were my pretence should I be discovered just being curious and wanting to find every inch of where I lived. And I found it. It is away at the back of the huge room where they entertain, it is found only by looking for it very hard.

A room which holds nothing but a beam with a hook in it, a table with straps attached, and many implements of which I am afeared and yet touched with longing excited fingers, implements which will burn and hurt and excite and thrill.

For now I must put them out of my mind. Serenia has not shown me the room nor must I confess to having found it.

Instead I will sit here and be glad of what I have. A small fire glows in the grate, I am warm and safe.

Dear sister, now I feel I am in the heart of London. How silly! With Alfred I lived in a huge Square where the elegant people came and went in high stepped hansom cabs drawn by high stepping horses, but here in Fleet Street it feels different. It is all bustle and colour, it is legal men in their flowing uniforms of black gowns and white wigs, alongside the men who write and prepare our newspapers. Or broadsheets as Cornelius prefers to call them, muttering over the news as he eats his breakfast of kippers, followed by kidneys, sausage, tomato, bacon, egg and ham. Yes, exactly the breakfast dear Papa consumes every morning, dear Sophie! Men are all alike, are they not?

Where the square is all elegance and ladies in expensive gowns, small dogs carried in muffs, parasols atwirl to keep off the sun and keep the skin a delicate shade of white, here it is busy busy busy. The Daily Telegraph thunders forth its Conservative words, the Daily News and Reader comes from Bouverie Street with its Liberal leanings, and oh so many provincial papers have their London offices here! Walk the pavements, look at the plaques on the walls, Aberdeen Free Press, Dundee Courier, Belfast Newsletter, intriguing names for me, dear sister, someone who had not ever left the country until the day I ran away and came here, to the heart of all that is living and breathing and wonderful in this fair land.

For there is life here!

Messenger boys run hither and thither, hansom cabs come rumbling by, omnibuses trundle around carrying their load of passengers, women walk in their elegant clothes and cheap clothes too, for not are all rich here, even though this be the richest city I know. There are poor beggar women who crouch on doorsteps and hold out an appealing hand for a coin. They do touch my heart so to see them, but for the Grace of Almighty God, that could have been me! Yet I have few coins to spare, I must save and save for my future. I fear to end up like them. But I give what I can to the most poor I see.

And all this I view from my eyrie, up here above Fleet Street. I can see across roof tops, I can hear the chime of St Bridgets Church and look at St Dunstans opposite the door, and there is St Pauls, so close by - if I were to walk along Fleet Street, through Ludgate Circus and up the other side there it would be in all its glory! Or so Serenia said when I asked. I will go, I will go, for there is much in my heart for which to thank our Almighty Father. I will go and set foot in that most hallowed of churches to give thanks for my new home.

Faith is still important to me, as is my Bible.

Oh yes, I must tell you how shocked Serenia and Cornelius were when they found out I could read and write! They did truly believe because I came from the country I had no education, forgetting of course that dear Papa is a Man of God and would not consider allowing his children not to be educated, they had to read their Bible daily!

It was like this. We were stood in this large and beautiful room with its huge ceilings and plenty of space such as I have never known for my own self, and I said

"Oh how beautiful it all is!" and Serenia said

"Yes, I hope you will have enough to do, dear Clarisse, for we will not always be with you."

I said without thinking

"But there is my Bible to read and my letters to write - " and the words were snatched from me and put into open shocked mouths.

"Read your Bible? Write letters?"

That was Cornelius looking as if I had just said I were descended from Queen Victoria herself and proved it!

And Serenia laughed and laughed until she could scarce stand.

"Oh my dear brother, I did believe we had a country bumpkin here, and all the time she is able to read! You will have to share your Times with her in the mornings!"

He scowled so fearful I was most afraid of him.

"My Times is not for sharing!" and he stomped off out of the room. Serenia smiled at me.

"My brother does wish so much to be the only person who can read and he will begrudge your reading. But I can think of a hundred ways to make it fun for the future - you can tell us about the time you had learning to read and write, I am sure you made many a mistake, and had many a punishment from your father and tutor, did you not?" and of course, Sophie, you and I did receive many a punishment, that is true.

So that is something to while away many a winter evening, for I have many a story to tell!

Then Serenia frowned in her turn.

"To whom do you write, Clarisse?" and it was said in a stern and hard voice. I faltered, and then said boldly

"My sister Sophie, but I cannot yet post the letters, for fear of my Papa finding out where I am."

"You use it as a Journal, I presume?" Serenia put her fingertips on my shoulders and I felt my usual thrill go through me.

"You are right, as always, Serenia."

"I know" and she kissed me very deeply. I felt myself go weak and wanting. "I will never ask you to reveal your letters to me, Clarisse, for we all need times and places to confess our thoughts and longings."

And she left me alone in my large room.

I would have been so happy, dear Sophie, so very happy, except for one small thing.

From downstairs I could hear Briggs' voice.

And I am sure, without knowing why, that he will play a large part in my future life.

CHAPTER 12

For almost a week Lauren had been in a fever of expectation. Judith had said nothing, hinted nothing, not even looked at her in a certain way to give Lauren any indication of what was going to happen. Nothing had been said but the address and the time. Her obedience to the order to go was implicit in the lack of instruction.

As the days progressed, Lauren had worked, but with only half her mind on the seemingly endless matrimonial disputes. The new Divorce Act had brought with it an influx of divorces, and an influx of new clients to cope with, while the original clients still demanded their time and attention. But Lauren was only aware of the ache in the pubis and the need to know what was going to happen, the desire, the overwhelming longing to submit to someone. All the time Judith hovered with a faint smile and a careful touch on the shoulder here and there, while Lauren ached to be held to be comforted to be TOLD.

The cool sharp evening had swept Fleet Street, fluttering litter and coats alike, fluttering her heart too as she hurried out to the street to hail a cruising black cab. As it pulled away from the kerb she strained her neck to see the windows of her flat, but the roof was too low and her own window too high. Lauren sat back, smoothing her seamed stockings with an eager hand, patting her long auburn curls, wondering if the sweater was too tight, should she have been less provocative, whether the skirt was too tight, would he want to remove it immediately, but knowing the lacy underthings were just right for they had been bought and approved by Judith just the week before.

Red. Bright screaming devil woman red.

Hailing and riding in a black cab was a thrilling act. It gave her a further sense of belonging, of being part of the metropolis, casually hailing a cab, giving an address, being accepted as a bona fide resident who knew where she had to go and took the quickest way of getting there.

The cab wove expertly among the cars, buses, lorries and other cabs cluttering London streets. Lauren stared out, admiring as she always did the graceful buildings, the tall golden trees now half bare as winter sent out its long enquiring fingers to find out whether they were ready for the cold. The large slender lamp posts looked down, casting their cold harsh light, so unlike that of the Temple where the gas lamps brought an olde worlde touch to a place which hadn't changed in a hundred years.

People bustled around, pre-theatre goers looking for dinner, for drinks, ladies wanting early customers, eager to get their earnings going, newspaper vendors calling their wares endlessly and almost inaudibly against the roar of London's traffic. Here there were homeless, snuggled into doorways with sleeping bags and blankets, with the glow of a handrolled cigarette warding off the night chill. There a man hustled a passer by for change, swearing, fists waving ineffectually against the night air as the man walked on without so much as a glance.

A girl with long blonde hair streaming from a bobble hat pulled fingerless mittens on to her hands and stared at the passing cab with open naked envy. Lauren felt her heart go into spasm. She had a home, she had comfort and security, money saved, good clothes to wear. Out there were homeless, beggars, young women like herself, young men with hopes and dreams shattered by the great impersonal City. When I walk past them again I'll drop some coppers into their hands, thought Lauren, wishing desperately she could stop the cab now, throw shillings at the girl, throw a pound note to the wind for any homeless person to catch, but the time edged on, her orders were to be there at seven. Her own skin had to be protected, her Master and Mistress obeyed.

The homeless would be there when she went by again.

"Here you are, Miss." The cabbie read the price from the meter, took her note and her "keep the change" with a smile and a mock salute. The cab roared off to look for another fare, another London resident with places to go and people to see.

The Square was cool, elegant and very fashionable, dripping money from its painted railings and elaborate window boxes and from the large expensive cars parked outside in the Residents Only marked out parking spaces.

A car drifted by, engine purring to itself as it shouted MONEY to the world. Birds hovered in the trees in the grass heartland, dried golden leaves whispered secrets as they tumbled round each other at the base of the trunks. Lauren checked the numbers on the first house and began to walk around the Square, aware of the passing time. At last, here it was.

A silver bright entry phone glared at Lauren as she walked up the clean swept steps, where not a leaf dared deposit its veins or its bright autumn colours, and where she felt as if she should have dusted off her shoes before setting a single foot on the pristine white.

As the hands of her minuscule watch swept toward 7 pm she pressed the buzzer for Grant.

"Lauren Sanderson," she whispered into the speaker box.

"Come up." The curt hard voice thrilled her again.

And the door opened. This was it. Realisation came with a sudden surge of emotion, of pure naked lust. For a moment she was ultra aware of the lines she carried, neat cane weals given to her by Judith, and wondered if they in turn would turn on Roger Grant.

The stairs were clean and carpeted, the plants fresh and green in the foyer. Lauren paused on the bottom stair, wondering what she was doing there, and then dismissed all doubts, firmly walking up each step, heels buried in the thick pile carpet. Luxury everywhere. And I thought I had a fine home, a penthouse suite atop one of Fleet Street's ancient buildings!

"There you are." Roger Grant stood in the doorway, as dark and glowering as he had seemed in Court, even without wig and gown, an imposing and solemn figure. "Come in."

"Thank you." Lauren dropped her coat on the chair he indicated. laid her bag on top of it and stood waiting, hands clasped before her.

"We'll go into the lounge." Lauren started after him. The lounge was magnificent, an Adam fireplace, a huge window with its comfortable padded seat, rich drapes, soaring ceiling with sculpted plaster work around the chandelier hook ...

Roger stood before the fireplace, hands behind his back. Lauren had a sudden vision of him wearing a velvet waistcoat with satin back, a huge gold watch chain holding it all together, imagined the tapestried bell pull with which he would summon -

"Has Judith said anything to you about why I asked you to come?"

"No."

"You don't ask many questions, I like that. Other subs who have been here have chattered on endlessly, what this why that what am I going to get - it bores me, that kind of idle chatter. Women usually bore me. Why I specialise in divorce work I'll never know, unless it is the thought of releasing men from those chattering inane women!" He turned a look on her back as black as the grate behind him. A grate which should hold a leaping fire of logs which would spit blue and purple flames, bright yellow sparks and a glowing red heat.

As glowing as I'm going to be.

"Undress." he told her suddenly. "I want to see you."

With his eyes burning holes into her skin, Lauren stood and as quickly as she could stripped off all her clothes, including the bright red undies. His expression didn't change, only the eyes smouldered harder than ever. She stood on the thick pile rug, her smooth pendulous breasts sagging very slightly, almost begging the hand to touch cup and hold them, her nipples standing proud with her excitement, begging a mouth to suck on them. Her hips flared out into the exciting roundness she knew only too well from her own explorations, her cheeks firm and waiting, marked with neat lines Judith had put there just a few days earlier. Her legs were long, shapely and strong, she stood on white delicate feet and waited, her hands clasped before her, just touching but not covering her pubis. Her tangle of hair matched her long auburn locks.

"Who caned you?" he asked, after he had walked around her twice. Lauren had blushed as his eyes took in all of her nakedness.

"Judith." A simple direct answer.

"Tell me about it." Roger sat down in a huge armchair, lit a cheroot, pointed a toe at her.

"I - now I live in a flat above the office in Fleet Street. Judith arranged it for me. She promised me I would have the cane the day I moved in, and I did."

"Tell me about it."

"There was little furniture." Lauren half closed her eyes, remembering. There was little furniture, for there hadn't been much time. That weekend she had loaded up her car with possessions, packed the boot so full with clothes, books and linen it would hardly close. Her typewriter, records and kitchen utensils had been stored on the floor at the back, on the back seat, on the shelf. In the passenger side Lauren had carefully placed her pot plants and precious ornaments. She had driven away from the caravan park without a single pang of sadness, had driven into London with a happy heart. It was as if it was all meant to be, somehow.

Then the whole lot had been unpacked and laboriously carried up the many flights of stairs into her flat.

Her home.

Judith had been busy, had acquired a bed, a chest of drawers, small bedside table, kitchen table, two armchairs and a table for the lounge, a bookcase and a cabinet to store her things. The fridge and washing machine would come later.

Lauren had unpacked as best she could in a hurry, not knowing when Judith was coming back. The ornaments and plants were in place, her clothes neatly put away, and the bed made, leaving only the books half arranged, when Judith finally walked in the door, carrying a large bag.

"All this can be stored up here now." She had tipped out the long thin cane, the two tawses which she favoured, a small efficient looking riding crop and a new purchase, a heavy duty paddle. "I promised you." Judith had smiled that knowing loving smile that turned Lauren over inside.

Without being asked, Lauren had slipped off her briefs and bent over the arm of the chair, presenting herself willingly to the woman she loved so much.

Judith had spanked her hard, six times, with the new paddle, raising red marks instantly. She stood back, admiring her handiwork, and then picked up the cane.

"I'll be gentle," she promised, hearing Lauren draw in an involuntary breath, but she had been hard and firm, six cuts that had Lauren shrieking in pain and astonishment. Despite the pain, unexpected and unbelievable, she had stayed there, gripping the worn armchair with both hands, white boned and rigid until Judith told her to stand up.

"Now, my darling girl" - Judith had run both firm hands over red lines - "now you will have something to take to Roger Grant on Wednesday."

"And so you have," he approved. "Kneel down." Lauren hesitated, looked around wondered where -

He was beside her in a single step, hand on the back of her neck, forcing her to the floor.

"I said kneel down!" The order this time was given this time with a stinging smack to both buttock cheeks.

Lauren knelt, head down, feeling both smacks burning, wondering what he had in store for her.

"Hands on the floor." Obediently she leaned forward, on all fours on his thick dusty carpet.

There was a long pause, and then he stood astride her, legs gripping her waist, facing backwards. She felt a stinging impact, a ruler? something hard and narrow, firmly applied. She bit her lip, taking the slaps that rained down on her exposed cheeks from a different angle, from top to bottom, covering the outthrust roundness but missing the tender curving overhang. No chance to wriggle or escape, his legs were like a vice, he had done this before. The spanking went on, burning, forcing unwanted cries into her throat, unwanted tears to the back of her eyes. He was harder and went on for longer than Judith had -

But Judith is new to this, she told herself, gripping the carpet, wondering if it would end, and what else she would have to endure.

Suddenly he stopped, left her burning and hurting kneeling on the carpet.

"Why are you here?" he asked, pulling her head back with long auburn hair. She looked at him, face red with the effort of not crying out.

"I am here because Judith told me to come."

"You aren't here for your own pleasure?"

Lauren considered her answer. "I am a submissive woman," she acknowledged at last, speaking softly and carefully. "But I am here because I am obeying Judith's orders."

"Good." He let her go, indicated a chair. "Sit down, I want to look at you."

Lauren sat, uncomfortably aware of the spanking she had received, eyeing the wooden ruler on the table with some concern. That was what had inflicted all this pain!

He stood before the fire again, reminding Lauren acutely of someone she must have seen, surely! He looked so - right - standing there. "I asked because I don't like submissive women. I don't like women! I don't like those who come because I am a Master, but say 'I only want to be spanked and nothing else' or 'don't hurt me too much'. You came because you were told to, you are a slave not a submissive. And that means I can beat you as hard as it pleases me and you will take it."

Lauren nodded, feeling the burning glow settling a little, but being matched with a surge of emotion stronger than that which swept through her when she first went to the front door. This is what she had read about over and over, in magazines and books, this was to be a full evening of pain!

"But you are relatively new," he went on, lifting a long heavy looking tawse from the table. Lauren wondered why she hadn't seen it before. "So I will be just a little lighter than usual, but, I still think, far harder than your Mistress has been." He indicated the armchair and Lauren stood up, feeling the redness sting and burn, leaned over the chair as she had done for Judith. She had hardly got her hands in position when the tawse landed, a thick burning band of pain and again, hard, not giving her time to breathe, again and again, and then he paused, leaving her gasping.

"This is new to you." He didn't wait for an answer, but gave her six stinging blows one after the other, making her throw back her head, cry out, cling to the chair. Again a long pause, time for the pain to settle, to make its way through to the sensitive parts of her. She was melting, longing. Another six and then he moved away, putting the tawse back on the table.

"Stand up." He touched her back. "You please me very much. You are not like other women, you do not fuss, cry out, deny you like it! You wait for instruction. A true slave, by nature more than by training. A jewel of a slave.

"Thank you." Lauren stood, hands clasped, head down, staring at her naked feet, wondering why they were so interesting to some people and so ugly to others. Previously she thought her feet were ugly but some had disagreed.

She was hurting. More than she had hurt before, more than she thought possible, a deep pain that still had within it an erotic thrill that was equal to nothing she had ever had before.

So far.

Tears rolled down her face, tears she did not try to wipe away.

A fine plaited dress whip in his hands, Roger Grant turned to her.

"Stand still." She did so while he whipped her swollen burning cheeks with pain so fine it cut like wire.

"Get dressed, go home." His final instructions. Slowly, tearfully, Lauren got dressed, easing her briefs over her bruised flesh, wondering how she might satisfy the burning desire that heated her through like an ember. He had no apparent bulge, no apparent sexual interest, and yet his eyes smouldered to match the heat in her own loins. Was that giving enough for him?

As she reached the door he stopped her with a touch so gently so featherlike she almost didn't feel it.

"Here." An envelope was thrust into her hand. She pocketed it with a tremulous smile. "Go home," he said in a gentle voice to match the touch. "Judith is waiting for you."

CHAPTER 13
NOVEMBER 1869

My dear Sister,

I have been remiss in setting my thoughts down on paper for a while but I have been occupied being lady of the house here in Fleet Street.

How things have changed since I left Alfred's dwelling! Now I am in complete control of this house, I have an allowance paid to the Bank each week, from which I draw what I need to pay the chimney sweep, the grocer, the butcher, the fishmonger, the baker and all else who come. I pay the tailor and seamstress for Cornelius and Serenia, and all other callers.

And most important of all, Sophie, and this you will find hard to believe, supervising the servant I have engaged to do the heavy cleaning work.

My wish to do something for the beggar women came true, well, for at least one of them. I found a young girl shivering on the corner of Farringdon Street, wearing no more than rags, offering to sell her body to the men who passed her by, yet drawing back in revulsion when one moved to take up her offer. I watched for a while, standing observing a shop window most delicately set out with ladies' apparel, the most beautiful deep edged crepe for mourning wear you have ever seen. Fortunate I am that I have no knowledge of my relatives, and have none to mourn so am not required at any time to go into black! I favour dark blue for my day dresses, with a white apron over the top, my hair caught back in a bun, very much a lady I am now!

Well, having watched the young woman for a while, and observing how she drew back from me, I approached her, Sophie, and invited her back for tea and warmth, and then found out her history.

Mary is a young girl, younger than I was when I ran away from home, but for different reasons. Her father welcomed the attentions of a much older man suing for her hand, while Mary herself found the idea so repulsive she said she would rather starve than submit to his embrace.

Of course, having got to the great City of London, she found starving was not a sensible idea after all, and was attempting to overcome her fear of men in order to live.

I know in my heart that this girl, this Mary, is one of the same mind as myself, she prefers the love of ladies, but refuses to admit it to herself or to anyone else. But in time she will come to it, in time, with love, with easement, with encouragement from Serenia and myself.

Serenia was delighted.

She came along one night, after a break of about a week. The carriage was driven by Briggs, the man whom I so fear. She came bustling in, beautiful in russet velvet gown and matching hat with huge golden feathers pluming from it.

"Clarisse?" As I came in she was stripping off her long warm gloves and tossing them on to the chair, standing by the fire which always burns in the grate in her chambers and Cornelius', whether they come or not. The room must be warm, the furniture kept in good condition, for the moment they arrive they need warmth for all that this November is mild and reasonably dry. There was a chill that night, a chill which City living can bring, and a fire is a good defence against the chill.

"I wish you to meet someone," I told her, ringing the bell by the fireplace. Mary came in, so neat and clean in her brown dress and neat white apron and cap. Serenia's eyes opened wide and she laughed aloud.

"Is this one of your waifs and strays, dear Clarisse? How delightful! Do come in."

I smiled, for Serenia knows my feelings about the beggar women all too well!

"This is Mary," I told her. "I found her starving on the corner of Farringdon Street and asked her to come and work here for food and lodging. She has one of my rooms."

Serenia took Mary's small delicate hands in hers and smiled into her eyes.

"Mary. Welcome to my home. My brother Cornelius will be pleased to see you here. There is just one thing you must know - we believe in discipline here, of the severest kind. Do you understand?"

"Yes Ma'am." Mary curtsied so prettily I was almost envious. She understood, dear Sophie, because I had explained it to her in great detail.

"We use the strap here a lot!" Serenia went on, smoothing Mary's trembling arms with her own fair hands. "If you hear the sound of someone being disciplined, do not come and look. Do you understand?"

"Yes Ma'am," Mary repeated, and her eyes, frightened and yet knowing, told us both she did.

I knew Mary's background, knew how her father had used his belt on her but did not tell Serenia any of this. It was best she find out for herself.

"Go to the kitchen," Serenia told her. "Briggs will be waiting there, and will want sustenance, find him some tea and some cold ham and cheese."

Mary curtsied again and left the room so silently it was a wonder either of us noticed her leaving. Serenia took me in her arms, and held me close.

"Oh my dear Clarisse, were you thinking you have been neglected and ignored? What a week it has been! We have foot and mouth among the cattle, and Cornelius has been frantic, trying every purge and cure he can find, and I have been consulting with the Estate Manager and others to find more workers for the estate. The nearby village has been depleted of able bodied people, and I wished for some other to come. Only now as I come into London and speak with you and our new shy Mary! do I see the answer to my problem! Only now do I see that like the Lord Jesus told us I should go out into the highways and byways and bring in the poor and the lame. Not that I will do that!" and her throat shone white in the firelight and candle glow as she laughed. "But I can find able bodied workers for our estate at no cost! I shall send Briggs out to find the able bodied beggars on the street and take them back to the country with us."

And then she grew serious, Sophie, oh so serious.

"Before then, my dear Clarisse, I have two tasks for you. One is to ensure that before I come again our new little shy Mary is fully broken to the instruction and the feel of the strap. You must do that, you must beat her for us until she learns to like it. And the second thing is, you must go to the room you have surely discovered by now" - I blushed for she had known my secret all along! - "And wait for Briggs and myself to come. Tonight he will beat you for me."

Briggs! My heart did grow cold in me, so cold, and yet underneath it a leap of feeling such as I have never known before, almost like the one I had before Papa came with the elders!

After much talk and some tea taken together, I went to the cold hard room for that is how I view it, a cold hard room. The walls are white, the beams black and the things which hang there defy description. I stood in the middle of this cold room, shivering, hugging myself with both hands, my loins afire with waiting and my nerves ajangle with the desire of it all.

At last they came, Briggs as foul looking as ever, as surly and as dark as ever, but looking well fed and sure of himself. For he had power in his hands, power to hurt, and that power was given to him by his Mistress, whom he clearly worshipped. I saw the way he looked, how he gave way to her, how he made obeisance to her and yet hungered for me with his eyes.

"Remove your pantaloons, Clarisse." Serenia was curt, hard, as she always is when we go into these acts. I removed my pantaloons and stood with my skirt around my waist, letting Briggs feast his eyes on me, saw them go dark and smoulder like fires. Here there is no fire, only the fire he will create and the fire I carry within me, and no doubt he in his loins.

Serenia did not ask me, but moved me back to the wooden bench and bent me over it, securing my hands to the other side. Then I heard her voice, heard the swish of her rich full velvet skirts, heard the rattle of the rack, heard Briggs move, his leather boots creaking as he stood in his place.

"Give her twenty Briggs, then twenty more and keep on until I say stop."

And my breath stopped in my mouth as the first stroke fell almost immediately. No chance to gather my thoughts my feelings my nerves together, it was a band of pain which had me shrieking like a thing possessed, hoping Mary would not hear and another fell and another and the first twenty were given without pause, leaving me sobbing helplessly in my bonds.

"Rest." The word was almost a command, and I heard his leather boots creak as he moved away. I had time to sob, to gather myself, to sense the pain shrieking round and through my emblazoned cheeks for sure they were on fire, as much as I was.

"This time slower" came Serenia's calm but hard voice and this time he was slower, an even paced twenty that had more impact coming over the first ones, and yet hurt less in some way for not being so fast.

And rest.

And another twenty, this time fast again, making me cry out in pure pain and need for him to stop.

And another rest.

And another twenty, slow again.

"Thank you, Briggs, I will do the rest" and Serenia came to stand by me. "Twenty more, my dear Clarisse, and you will have taken an hundred strokes. How does it feel to know you are now the proud possessor of a behind so badly punished it is on fire and speckled here and there with blood weals? And that you will have taken an hundred strokes in the name of love for me?"

And I melted under the words, under the touch of her cold white hand, under the sting of the strap as she swung it over and over again on my punished cheeks.

A hundred!

Never before have I taken so many, never has it hurt so much.

"And now - " I had thought Briggs to be gone but he was still there, for the boots creaked again, a hand was thrust between my legs, my thighs spread and a cock hard and long and rough - how can such a smooth thing be rough? thrust into me.

Briggs!

No doubt fulfilling every dream of his to fuck me as I lay helpless and beaten before him.

And Sister of mine, it may be sin and depravity, it is likely to be the worst thing that Papa could envisage, to be punished and enjoy it but it was good. Very good.

It was at that moment - of all moments to choose! - as she untied my hands and caressed me and dismissed Briggs, did Serenia choose to whisper to me that she had arranged for my portrait to be painted, and I was to wear the green velvet riding suit. She wanted to take it back to the estate, to be reminded of me when I was not with her.

Your sister in a portrait! Can you imagine, dear Sophie, how that thrilled me? More than the beating, more than the fucking, more than the touch of her hand that thrills me beyond all sense and reason.

Only Society ladies get their portraits painted, and I was to be framed in gold!

CHAPTER 14

"In here Mr Williams." Lauren led the way into her flat, unnecessarily showing the caretaker where the bathroom was. She blushed and apologised. "I tend to forget you know this place better than me!"

"Don't worry about it, Miss Lauren, you're being polite, more than I can say about some young woman!" He lifted the cistern lid and leaned over it, poking and prodding at the rusting mechanism inside. "Yes, needs a washer and perhaps a new arm on there, see what I've got downstairs." He stood up, eased his back and looked at her.

"Like I said you're one of the polite ones. Some of them girls want their arses tanned, that they do! Excuse my French. Good leathering with a belt would do them a lot of good, and by God I'd give it to them if I could! Now you, Miss Lauren - " he made his way to the hall and put a hand on the door lock - "you act as if you've had that good tanning! Won't be long." He walked out, leaving Lauren a little shaky, and a little embarrassed, as if he had walked in and discovered her with a vibrator.

She went back to her lounge and sat down in the big comfortable armchair, leaving the front door on the latch for Mr Williams to come back up and fix her overflowing cistern. There would be towels to wash later, the ones she had used to mop up the water. She realised she was trying not to think.

"Hi, Lauren?" Judith appeared in the doorway, smiling but looking puzzled, holding a dripping umbrella in one hand and something wrapped in paper in the other. "Did you expect me? Only the door was open."

"No, I didn't." Lauren got up and went over to give Judith a kiss and took the umbrella from her to put in the sink. "I'm waiting for Mr Williams, he's fixing the cistern for me right now." She hurried to the kitchen,.

When she came back Judith handed Lauren an African violet in bloom in a ceramic pot.

"I thought you'd like this."

"Oh I do, it's lovely, thank you!" Lauren put it on the end of her cabinet, moved a clown ornament and stood that on the mantelpiece. Judith watched her.

"I know this is a silly question but - is there some reason you've not hung anything over that fireplace yet?"

"Well yes." Lauren turned slowly, looked at the empty space and grinned a little shamefacedly. "I'm looking for the right picture."

"You've prints galore, girl, what's the matter with them? Or a large mirror? That one in the hallway, that oval thing in the oak frame, that would look good there!"

"No, there's a certain picture I'm waiting for." Lauren could not explain further, she just knew the picture she wanted, and she hadn't yet found it.

"Here we are - hello Miss Brooks, good to see you again. Just got a small job to do here for Miss Lauren."

"So I see, keeping you busy already, Mr Williams."

"Not Miss Lauren, no, she don't ask for a thing, right polite sort of person she is."

"I should hope so! I keep her in line, you know, Mr Williams, give her a good hiding now and then!"

"I wouldn't be surprised if you did either, Miss Brooks." It was said with a laugh and a look that said 'don't tell me such stories'. "Funny that, we was talking afore you came about girls what needed their arses tanned, excuse my French, I was saying to Miss Lauren here how she acted like she had it done to her! Won't be long, just get this done and then we'll get the water turned back on for a brew of tea."

"There's a hint if ever I heard one!" Lauren went back to the kitchen to prepare the cups, glad she had been able to escape the embarrassing conversation.

It hadn't been embarrassing, she realised. Just awkward, just touching too many nerves in her body. She reached for a packet of biscuits, put them on a plate, stood surveying the walls, decorated with fancy tea towels.

Who lived here before I did? I mean, not recently, but years ago when this was a house? Surely it was a house? It had big beautiful rooms - the high ceilings are still there, and the delicate plaster work, even if it was hidden under layers of paint and plastered over cracks. Each floor was probably a suite of room, large and beautiful, probably expensively furnished and decorated. The huge windows would have had rich velvet drapes, there would have been fine upolstered furniture, elaborately carved furniture, fancy lamps and gas mantles, no doubt. And here would have moved -

A woman. A beautiful woman, with tight curls and long flowing gowns, full skirts to swish quietly around the floors with thick rugs.

"Day dreaming?" Judith came into the kitchen, slipped an arm around her waist, pulled her close.

"Sorry, yes I was, wondering who lived here, years ago."

"Oh it was a rich home, I understand." Judith smiled at her. "Some very rich family owned it, when they died it was no doubt sold off and then converted to offices. I know what you mean, there's something elegant about the sweep of the staircase, the plastered ceilings."

"I'm glad you noticed too, it wasn't just me."

"OK, ladies, the water's back on again!"

Lauren pressed the switch on the kettle. "I'm very happy here," she told Judith on impulse.

"I know. It shows, which is probably why there's a tinge of jealousy among the staff. But none of them needed a home, there's no reason for them to be jealous, except that it's Stella's nature."

Mr Williams appeared in the doorway, lean, almost desperately thin, his face solemn even as his eyes smiled.

"Have to see about that wall of yours one of these fine days, Miss Lauren, there's mould growing up, back of the bath. But it'll be all right for a bit longer. I'll have to get permission off the owners to see to it for you, in case it turns out to be a big job. I'll get on to that in the morning."

"Thank you, Mr Williams. The tea won't be long."

"Ah, right nice of you to make some tea, Miss Lauren." He walked away to the lounge, leaving them smiling.

"As if he hadn't asked!" Judith picked up the plate of biscuits. "I'll go keep him company."

Later, when the caretaker had left, promising again to see to the wall, Judith held out her arms.

"Come, it's a long time since I did what I'm longing to do, give you a long slow hand spanking."

The talk of people being punished with a belt had stirred Lauren's senses, and even though she had pushed the thought down, it had remained like a burr in her mind. Knowing that Judith was there for longer than a flying visit had added to her feelings, she had known something was coming, known that the evening would end in a session of some kind or another. She had been walking wet with excitement for what felt like ages, but in reality was no more than half an hour.

It was difficult to repress the sensation of being ridiculous, lying across someone's knees, feeling large and awkward, feeling slightly ludicrous, but then the spanking started. From the first slap, hard and firm on a soft cheek, Lauren knew it was to be a long session, and resettled herself, hands on the floor, toes on the floor, eyes closed, feeling the emotions surge through her, pain/pleasure so deeply linked there was no telling them apart, no parting them!

Harder now, firmly covering all her skin, the slaps overlaying, the pain deepening, Lauren aware of Judith's musk, the womanly smell that hung around her faint as a summer breeze on a hot night.

Outside the rain fell steadily, coating Fleet Street in water, hissing against the windows, complementing, a background to the incessant slaps raining down on her exposed cheeks, no doubt flame red now under Judith's ministrations, sending more and more quivers of excitement and interest through her.

"OK, up you get." Lauren stood, clutching both cheeks as she always did, knowing no amount of massage would ease the pain, not wanting it to, wanting it to last.

There was an unspoken invitation to go to bed, and they went, rolling around together in an ecstasy of loving that lasted almost as long as the glow from the spanking.

Outside the rain fell, washing away the litter and dirt, chilling the air, sending everyone scurrying home for safety and warmth.

Lauren safe and warm, considered herself the luckiest person in London. And wondered whether the long gone people who lived there before felt the same.

CHAPTER 15
DECEMBER 1869

M y dear Sister,

Tonight it is raining.

The rain is falling from heavy dark clouds, there is no moon, no stars, no light. I feel restless, and having bid Mary to watch over the house - she sitting by a tiny fire in her room where she sleeps and lives, I have given up my small room for her, you see, dear Sophie, even as you would to someone who needs a home.

For all that it is wet I betook myself out, down the many flights of stairs and out into Fleet Street to walk along the wet pavements to hear the huge presses rumbling like underground monsters roaring to be free. Here and there a messenger hurried by clutching papers, a jacket pulled over their heads, or a cap dripping moisture down their backs. I walked with the smell of London in my mind, the heaviness of so many people, the printing ink, the paper cut and stored, horses, people, and here and there a hint of the country, a softness, a smell of greenery from a garden somewhere, or a tree giving up its night scents to the world.

And I longed with all my heart to walk the roads near our home, to see the stars, the moon hanging low and light, the silhouettes of trees, to hear the night animals, the bark of a fox, the nightjar, the owl! I did long to see golden squares casting light on to vegetable patches and not cold streets where beggars huddle in doorways and look beseechingly at us who pass by.

Oh, the beggars, dear Sophie, wet and cold, for it is cold in London for all that the buildings are heated and the great presses do give off their own heat as they work! The chill is enough to penetrate even the thick shawl I wore over a thick skirt and many petticoats to keep me from the cold, how these people live in their poor rags I do not know. I do wonder at how they should live such a life.

Remember this, dear Sophie. For all that Papa will have taken a switch to you or a strap, for all the times you have suffered at his hands, and maybe now you are of age you will be thinking of marrying and give yourself to a husband who will also beat you, for are not all men that way inclined? You have at least a home.

Fear not that you will not be able to take the sting of the strap, for surely we women can always take the strap! Are we not given by God the roundness the firmness the ideal things for others to use their strap on? Our buttocks are asking for a hand, a switch, a strap, a birch! And I for one rejoice that I am so blessed, for I do dearly love the sting and the glow that comes later, when it translates itself into the thrill of deep deep longing, and that thrill to be answered by a touch of fingers and a touch of lips and tongue!

I did not think to long so much for home, but the rain, the glistening pavements, the smells, it brought reminders of home and I longed for the scent of fresh washed earth, chill under winter skies, knowing all was not dead but hibernating, awaiting the touch of Spring. It took much thought and a few tears to make me put aside such thoughts to make me not go home to pack a bag and catch a train back to you, for I could do it now, I have money aplenty and could outface Papa any day. It came to me in a rush that Christmas will soon be here, and I am very much afraid of having Christmas alone.

Then I realised I walked alone and unafraid, I who used to tremble at the sound of a footstep coming near.

I know now most are law abiding people going about their business, but for all that I carry no reticule or money on me, it is all safely stored in Messrs Coutts & Co. and I knew I had become a city person all through. I was truly delighting in the thud of the presses, the rush of the messengers, the sound of the policeman about his business, this is the rhythm of my life,

I have to tell you this. My portrait is done. How grand it looks too, in its gold frame! I have to hope Serenia likes it as much as I do. Somehow the artist has caught my look, a sort of mischievous sparkle, and a hint of a smile. The green velvet riding suit was a perfect choice, it frames my curls and face, and gives me the look of a lady.

Oh how vain this looks on paper! But how proud I am to be in a portrait! How grand it felt to leave here in my day clothes, carrying my riding suit and go visit the artist in his room, near Blackfriars, a small room smelling of spirit and paint, brushes left in jars everywhere, and the scattering of canvasses round the wall. It made me feel - a little inadequate at first, for here was a man with skills I could never possess, but he soon talked to me and put me at my ease, trying me here and there, until we decided on the gold drapes at the back to offset the green and the red in my hair. Then I would go behind the screen he had to carefully erected, and put on the green suit for the sitting. It took many visits, oh indeed, many visits, until he was satisfied, but now I am captured forever in paint.

And I will grace the walls of Serenia's rooms in her country home, even more grand, do you not think?

One day, dear sister, I will post these letters to you so you know what your sister Clarisse has been doing here in the sinful city of London!

What have I been doing, you will ask? Apart from having my portrait painted, I have been left alone, neither Cornelius or Serenia has set foot in London Town for some weeks, while I trained my servant Mary into the ways they would like.

I did it carefully, you can be sure!

Here and there, transgressions, a floor left unwashed, a dress not put away, a cabinet left unpolished, I would call her in the evening to account for her errors of the day. How small how still he stood, her long straight hair tumbling out of the bun in to which she wound it every morning, and which I refused to let her tuck back, for she looked so innocent with the strands of hair around her face, so adorable, I could love her myself.

I do.

Yet it is in my mind that Serenia and Cornelius will wish to love this girl, this beauty, and Cornelius do like a virgin so I must take care to present her to him as virgin.

Punished at first with a leather slipper, resounding smacks against the small cheeks, bringing up the redness, making her cry out and squirm and wriggle, yet holding her down with a hand around the waist as she lay helpless over my knees and later with the strap - I learned the thrill of domination. Was this in Serenia's mind when she gave me the orders, that I would learn to thrill to dominate as well as submit?

After one spanking one night I asked Mary if she had heard me under punishment that night, and she confessed she had. I guessed by the brightness of her eyes and the flushed face that she was beginning to enjoy the discipline, and her admission she had listened as I had been beaten confirmed it. I asked her outright

"Did it please you here and here" pointing to her pubis and her heart "to hear me strapped so hard?"

"That it did," she confessed, her eyes aflutter, her eyelashes laying like secrets along her fair cheeks.

I placed her down on the carpet and pushed up her clothes, and she let me, her eyes sparkling in the candle light. I touched her secret button and felt her explode in ecstasy and my own loins fired as a result of that. Then I sent her to her room, knowing I had won, that she would be good to touch to beat to subdue when my Master and Mistress came again.

And I went to my own room with a candle, and instead of lighting it I slid it into my wet waiting place and came and came and came.

CHAPTER 16
DECEMBER 1969

As darkness crept over London, flattening the street lights so they appeared hooded, crushing the glow from the windows so they appeared half lit, Lauren had yielded to an urge she hadn't fully understood, put on a thick coat and for the first time since she had moved in, went walking London streets.

Wine bars and pubs threw the most cheerful light out on to the pavements, glistening dark tarmacadam reflecting distortions of life, much as drink distorted the view of life.

Shop windows boasted bright decorations and Christmas goodwill messages, beneath the glitter the unspoken urgent message - buy buy buy. Lauren looked in windows, wondering what to buy Judith, what did you buy someone so masterful, so strong, so - capable?

From a church the sonorous sounds of an organ, the flicker of the sanctuary light, splashes of colour mixed with the glow of the street lamps. From doorways the sound of breathing, of a ragged cough, a cigarette being lit, the glow of a firefly dancing in the darkness. A siren, shrieking through the black, cutting it through, slicing the silence into chunks, the silence that only a city can give, a heartbeat of people, traffic, machinery, trains thundering underfoot and planes roaring overhead. Through it all the silence could be found, here, in Temple, where the stones were worn by countless feet, where gas lamps shed a Dickensian glow, where walls held mysteries they could not reveal.

Here ran the Thames, rippling with light, rippling with cold, the barges and pleasure boats vying for space under the bridges. Here the lights were fairytale, strung out along the bridges, reminding her of Never Never Land reminding her of the city, an ordinary place by day an exciting and a different almost magical place at night.

I wonder who else has walked these street at night, she mused, clutching her coat tight around her neck, stopping cold draughts from penetrating her inadequate clothes. Who else has walked here, looked at the river, despaired of finding a life a love and a future?

I have life, and love, and a future.

She had turned back to her flat then, walking firm on the stones, stepping past the homeless crammed in the doorway, murmuring her apologies, she made her way inside, locking and bolting the door against the vagrants, glad to be out of the cold.

As it had the first time she had entered the building, it seemed to reach out, to wrap itself around her. The stairs beckoned, guiding her upwards. Here, first floor, what had been here? Some man's suite of rooms, complete with rich drapes and manly leather covered furniture? Did he pore over maps here on the seven seas or in the City night, did he plan a future life on the seven seas or in the city itself, wheeling and dealing in gold stocks and shares?

Second floor, what had been here? Did a woman live here, or did they entertain here, for surely they entertained, all Society people entertained!

She climbed higher, past the offices now firmly locked against intruders for the night, the only intruder her shadow falling across the frosted panels. The security lights came on and off she passed, as if she were a magician weaving her spell to make light and lose light.

When she came to her own flat she went inside, locked and bolted the door, and stripped off her clothes. She lay flat on the bed, gazing up at the ceiling, clutching two vibrators, one white and slim and feeling as if it was pulsing with power in her legs, gripped a nipple between two fingers, and began to fantasise.

I am walking along the road, an address in my mind, aware of being on time, for surely you must be on time to visit a mistress.

Here, this is the house, with neat railings and manicured garden, with beautifully cared for wooden door and glittering brass knocker and letter box. This is it. My nemesis my pain my dues.

My fluttering nerves can surely be heard a hundred yards away! The dryness of my mouth, the dampness of my palms, the wetness of my quim, oh why am I walking here, what am I doing here, what is the matter with me, walking toward pain?

The door opens as if by magic, why do I always assume - forget it concentrate here touch here under the breast here, where the cheek curves toward the thigh so soft so real so - feminine. Touch myself feel the lips quiver feel their wrinkled wetness feel their sensitivity how easy it would be to hurt myself to press to squeeze to send pain shivering through me.

What would it be like to be pierced there, to have someone - Judith - pull on the ring, to have something attached to the ring, weights - oh the flutter of feelings as I feel myself! Oh sense the sensations squirming through me as I slowly stroke myself with the throbbing vibrator!

She is there, my mistress. She is wearing a simple white dress, no sleeves, low cut showing her ample shapely breasts. The dress clings, I see the outline of her hips, the outline I know so well, the sweep of bone into the pelvic region, the cluster of curls at her mound, and I long to touch to caress to taste but no, that is not why I am here.

Why I am here us a different thing entirely.

"Come!" and I follow, for I always do in my fantasies and I do in real life also, I follow.

A dungeon. A playroom, she calls it, a room with padded benches and horses to bend over, straps for suffering and mirrors to see. And racks of implements of pain and pleasure awaiting my skin my skin my skin.

With one swift fluid movement my mistress strips off the white dress and stands in silver bikini skintight and concealing nothing. Her nipples are erect at the thought of dealing with me. She detests men yet deals with them daily, for money. Detests them for the pain they bring to women. Yet it is in disciplining women she finds her pleasure, and she brings all her skills to the punishment sessions.

Over her knees, her cool skin on mine for I am stripped to nothing to be sure she misses no part of me she wishes to hurt. Over her knees feeling childish and waiting for the sting of whatever she chooses, never her hands, her white hands are not allowed to touch someone, she prefers to use something hard and inflexible usually. Now, a paddle. Flat and hard, it covers a wide area, it smacks on this cheek and that and I gasp and writhe and she orders me to be still and I am. Again and again, the paddle, flat hard unyielding crushes the flesh stings the skin raises redness and sharp pain that makes me gasp and cry out and disobey the order to be still.

Over a padded bench, hands secured to the legs, ankles secured to each other, helpless, cannot balance, must lean forward, must throw the body weight into the bench as she has designed it to do. Helpless. Bottom red and stinging, helpless I await the tawse, her favourite, a three tailed heavy one that is well used, flexible, well able to deliver a violent and nasty sting, as it does now. She gives twelve from one side, twelve from the other. I know the drill, she has done it before. Twelve times standing to my right, the thickness of the leather and delight of the leather wrapping itself around me covering both cheeks at once, covering the stinging redness of the paddle, covering the skin making me cry out for release and yet delighting in the pain, for the pain goes deep and touches every feeling I have. Thrills and spills - thrill of anticipation and apprehension of fear and longing and spill of juices which are oozing and she knows it.

Repeat, twelve times standing to my left, the leather wrapping itself over the weals already inflicted, crying out and protesting and getting nowhere for the twelve will come whether I want it or not, and I do want it, of course I do, it is my desire, my feeling, my own decision to be there.

I am allowed to rest to wait to stand to rub and to ease the pain a little before the cane, oh twelve hard nasty cuts with a fine whippy cane are enough and then and then and then -

The vibrator in my slit, deep, deep, throbbing, the small one in my hand, rolling around the lips, touching the clit with buzzing angry head, thrusting deep deep inside slick with wetness, slick with my own wetness, in and out again rolling around and around, one here one there buzzing throbbing touching, sliding, sliding down the inner thighs back around the hair, touching, tormenting, teasing, finding the clit again bringing it erect in its tiny hood touching and sliding and ramming deep deep inside again and back out and around and touching and sliding and buzzing and awakening, until the feelings rush toward the great climax and the vibrator buzzes silently inside touching all the nerves all the nerves all the nerves -

"Is it never going to stop raining?" Judith edged in to Lauren's flat, carrying a large package. "I got soaked this morning and I'm going to get soaked on the way home too!"

"I'm so lucky to be living upstairs, it's just not true!"

Judith followed Lauren into the lounge, still carrying the package.

"You never did tell me, did you get rid of the car all right?"

"Yes, I did, the money's safely stored in the bank."

"Good. You'll need all you can get one day. If you want to go on living alone, that is. Here, early Christmas present."

"Already?"

"Why not? I can't keep the damn thing in my place, it's not big enough, and anyway I don't want to take it home and then bring it back again."

As Judith talked, Lauren undid the gift, carefully picking undone the knots and balling the string. She had a sense of what the parcel contained, it was as if someone had told her in advance what it would be. Large, square, heavy.

"Cost me a fortune," Judith mumbled, but with a smile, the happiest Lauren had seen her for some days. "No, not really. It came up at charity auction near home, I felt I had to buy it."

A portrait. Gold framed, a girl with laughing eyes and auburn curls, wearing a green velvet suit. Exactly the right picture to go over the fireplace.

To hide her overwhelming pleasure, Lauren jested: "You really couldn't bear to see that empty wall, could you?"

"No I couldn't! And somehow I knew this would be right. Is this the picture you've been looking for?"

"It is." And for a moment there was a third presence in the room, an indefinable someone smiling on them both.

"It's too heavy for a single nail, so I'll ask Mr Williams to come and put a proper big hook in for you. That all right?"

"Thank you. Thank you so much!" Lauren impulsively hugged Judith, and kissed her. "You couldn't have bought me a finer present."

"Good. Then you won't mind agreeing to the proposition I've been made, will you?"

"Tell me." Lauren looked at the smiling laughing eyed girl in the portrait.

"Roger Grant, he wants to stage a mock trial with you as defendant. I'm supposed to be defending you. If we lose, well, if you lose! you get - well, thrashed, frankly. He's asking some of his higher up legal friends and people from Chambers, people he knows are into the scene. Are you willing?"

"Yes." Said fast, and then again "yes" very slow and serious. "Yes, I am."

"Look, I'm sorry, I've not been near or by you, have I? I've been grumpy and horrid lately, but I've been - "

"With a man."

"Well, yes and he dropped me at the end of the week. I feel - dirty."

"I love you." Lauren spoke with certainty, knowing the words were sincere, knowing too they had come from the girl in the portrait, the girl with the curls.

"Do you? Do you really? Come, prove it to me."

Lauren went willingly into Judith's arms.

CHAPTER 17

My dear sister,
It is Christmas Eve, no, the clocks are striking the hour, the clocks across London, sonorous, almost funeral tolling. One am. Christmas Day.

I feel -

Content.

A fire flickers in the grate, which is black leaded to perfection by Mary, flames reflecting in the blackness. On my table, thick covered with fringed cloth, is a bright shining paraffin lamp, the glass chimney directing the heat and light to the ceiling where a heavy lamp hangs from gold chains. Under my feet, a warm rug. I am wearing a new shawl, soft as a dream at Midsummer, a gift from Serenia and Cornelius. Mary has a fire in her room, and is murmuring of the dinner we will eat tomorrow, such as a feast, for we have bought hams and sausages by the pound, puddings and desserts light enough to melt in a sinner's mouth, all from the market.

Mary says she has never been content before but tonight as she dozes and nods her way through the evening she is content.

Christmas Day will be more special, for I have invited Alfred to come for dinner. Yes, dear Alfred, whom I have not seen since the day I left his house for this fine home, an Alfred much down on his luck and taking meals where he can, it is said. I sent an invitation, with Serenia's blessing, for they will be in their country home with friends from nearby homes. Christmas would have been Mary and I alone but I thought to ask Alfred and the speed with which the messenger brought the answer told me I had done the right thing.

I have been to church, as I promised you so long ago in letters I would, set foot across the doorway and entered the huge soaring wonderland of St Pauls Cathedral. Candles flickered, everywhere, and the spirit of our Lord was surely with us, as it was with His mother on that day so long ago. The service was long and sonorous as befits such a splendid place, and yet lifted my spirits in a way no service has done before, the words of the preacher inspired me as Papa's words have never done.

I have a special reason to be feeling content tonight. I bear Cornelius' child. I have told him, yes of course I have! He professes to be thrilled, has promised to give the child his name, for all that it will be born a bastard. If it is registered in his name it will have a chance of inheritance, of standing in society and life.

So your sister sits here, a staid lady tending to plump with a child in her womb, feeling as if the world is hers!

And indeed, tonight it is.

CHAPTER 18

Dear Mum and Dad,

Christmas Eve, and Fleet Street remains bustling and lively, home going reporters and print workers, late office workers and occasional night people. I've been out today, buying last minute things for my Christmas dinner. I won't be alone, I've asked my boss Judith Brooke, as she was so good in getting me this flat.

I know you're disappointed I haven't made it to Spain for Christmas this year, but I've not been able to get the time off, we've had a lot of illness at work, and some heavy cases which have kept us at the office for hours. I'll try and make it in January, a winter holiday in the sun. I'll phone and let you know as soon as I know I can arrange the time.

My flat looks really lovely, I've decorated it for Christmas, a small tree, some lights, a few Santas and tinsel, a bit of holly and ivy, coloured balls, very pretty it all looks, very festive. I added red candles to the mantelpiece, they flicker on the painting -

I don't think I told you about that. I've been looking for a painting for some time, but not just any old painting, a certain one. Judith kept laughing at me, saying I had plenty of prints to put up but they weren't right. I knew what I wanted, and she found it for me, in a local charity auction. It's my Christmas present from her, a portrait of a girl with laughing eyes, wearing a green velvet suit. I think they used to call them riding outfits. Something like that. Anyway, Mr Williams, the caretaker, put a huge hook in the wall for me with epoxy resin to hold it in place and we hung the portrait.

"Looks a rare treat, Miss Lauren," he said in his funny old fashioned courteous way. "It looks - right." He's absolutely right, it does, as if it were meant to be there. It's a beautiful picture of a beautiful girl/woman. I'm not sure how old she is, she looks young, and yet old in the eyes, as if she knows the world and all it can throw at her, and has come to terms with it. I like that.

Add the candles and the face comes alive. I have no doubt the girl in the picture lived with candles, and perhaps those paraffin lamps, something that would add to a glow to the face, not the cold electric light we live with!

Listen to me, poetic tonight, aren't I? That's the feel of Christmas in the air, the cold tinge to the wind, the bite of frost in the morning, and the flurries of rain which feel like snow and I could almost kid myself it is snow.

How you can have Christmas in the sunshine I just don't know, it wouldn't feel the same!

Is there going to be a Christmas service at the local church, I wonder? and will you go?

I did something special, and went to the late service in St Pauls. It felt odd at first, being a normal worshipper in something which is usually on the tourist trail, but it is after all a parish church, serving people who live in London, and I loved every moment of it. The solemnity of the service, the feeling of being where others had worshipped for so many years, to come out into a London lit by many lights and humming with life, rumble of trains, rumble of aircraft flying people to holiday destinations or to join their relatives, for a moment I felt homesick for you both, and your flat out there in Spain but once the door closed behind me and the lights flicked on and the glow of the Christmas tree met me I knew I had come home in an odd sort of way.

I'm thinking of getting a budgie; it would be something to come home to, wouldn't it? Only problem is, who could take care of it while I came to visit you?

but I could always ask Mr Williams, he lives not far from here.

I must ask him one of these days why he didn't live here! It's a lovely flat.

I can't post this until after Christmas, there is no collection of mail until then, but I wanted to sit and write to you tonight, while I feel so happy. The clocks across London are striking one, and I feel -

The oddest affinity with the past. Don't laugh, it's your daughter being fanciful, or the influence of the painting.

The main thing is, for the first time in a long time, I feel content.

CHAPTER 19
NEW YEAR'S DAY 1870

My dear Sister,

What I wonder would Papa make of the scene we enacted here last night!

No doubt he would have had a fit, have ordered me for immediate clerical flogging and I would have been thrashed to within half an inch of my life. Oh how many times I think of Papa and his beatings, his diet of punishment and retribution, none of which made any difference to my rebellious nature and wayward spirit! Yet I do dwell on them at times when I am alone and there is a candle not lighting my room. Not that Serenia or Mary or Cornelius know anything of that.

First let me tell you how Cornelius and Serenia are taking care of me! A careful diet has been planned, wine diluted with water, no tea coffee or spices, just plain boiled vegetables and sensible food. Mary is to supply me with all this, along with the order for a rest every afternoon and early to bed. Mary does the very heavy shopping too, leaving me just the light things to carry and then I am ordered to take a hansom or growler back to the house. So you can be sure all is well with me. I feel well, none of the sickness some women are plagued with, I well remember dear Mama being so sick with the last baby whom I hope and pray did recover.

And gifts, oh my sister the gifts! Comes a shawl fine enough to fit into my hand, bundles of elaborately beautiful baby clothes, a ring set with a garnet, a pendant, a hat with delicate and elaborate plumes, so many things for the woman who carries a child for Cornelius!

I protest, oh yes, I protest, saying no one knows if I will go to term and deliver a healthy child but Cornelius and Serenia are sure enough that they continue to ply me with gifts.

I must rest, be strong and be well for their sake.

Why, you are asking, has Cornelius showered such blessings on me? Alfred, dear Alfred, gave me the answer after dinner over port, at Christmas time.

Cornelius, he said, was once married to a flighty pretty girl who was delicate as a summer afternoon and just as passing for she died as soon after the wedding he hardly had time to change out of his fine clothes. It is rumoured he tried some of his discipline on her and she died under it, but others say she bore a child and died because of it and the child too. I cannot say which is true, both might be for all I know! But I do know this, Cornelius and Serenia are as delighted over this child as if it were their very own, for have I not said how they act as if they are married? So close they are, so fine a brother and sister, much as we were once upon a time. Oh Sophie, it is times like these I miss you such!

And why has Serenia not married? Because other than Cornelius she cannot bear the touch of a man upon her skin in any way.

So there you see the picture clear. Cornelius needs an heir and is looking for a son. He has never found another woman to marry, it is said, despite many offers of eligible women from neighbouring families with daughters to marry off.

Am I without shame? Papa would say so. I know this. I am as married to Cornelius as if we had been married before God and man in a church somewhere for we are close, and I know his thoughts.

Cornelius has said all pleasures must cease. This for me is hard, so very hard! But again it is something I look forward to later, when the child is here, and my body is back to normal.

In the meantime there is Mary.

I come back to how it started.

What I wonder would Papa make of the scene we enacted here last night! No doubt he would have had a fit, I would have been thrashed to within half an inch of my life. The way I feel right now I would welcome it.

Serenia and Cornelius arrived in their carriage, driven by Briggs, that surly dark man whose presence bothers me. Briggs had no doubt been primed as to his moves, for he spoke not a word to them nor they to him, yet it went like syrup poured over griddle cakes.

We were all in Cornelius' rooms, a fire burning bright, lamps lit, candle burning, glowing, filling the room with light and deep red richness of warmth and luxury. Outside there was the sound of revellers, for the New Year was almost upon us.

Cornelius stood with his back to the fire, so strong, so tall, so beautiful I loved him even more in that moment.

"We are gathered together for the New Year celebrations" he said, looking at each of us in turn, Mary, Briggs, Serenia and myself. "For each, a gift that they will remember. Mary, tonight your gift to me will be your maidenhead, but first you will submit to Briggs for discipline of his choosing, that is my gift to him. He is a fine and loyal servant and deserves a gift. From that you will receive your gift, the pain you crave, and the giving up of your childish body to become a woman. My sister's gift is to watch. Clarisse, your gift too is to watch, for I cannot allow anything to harm my child! but later oh my dear girl, later I will discipline you, for you will be in need of it, sore in need of it!

by the time our child arrives! For now believe me my gift is the child you carry and the pleasure you will get from watching."

Before the fire Mary carefully removed her petticoats and skirts, and turned her back to Briggs, showing him her neat rounded cheeks that I had seen and punished so often, but he had never seen them before. The firelight flickered on the cool ivory white skin, so soon to turn red! And she smiled at me as she turned, for she knew her gift was one worth having. Her eyes sparkled with pleasure.

Briggs had a birch with him, a long whippy birch, wet and flexible. I had never been birched, my body cried out with longing to feel the sting, the bite of the many twigs he had bound together. Mary found the footstool Cornelius used and laid down over it, leaving nothing but candlelight and firelight to show him her deep shadowy crevice and most secret place. He walked over to her and without a word began to birch her. She was low down, he had all the swing he needed to bring the birch down with great strength, giving her in all thirty-six strokes, making her cry out, kick up her legs and grip the legs of the stool with hands that went white with tension but true to her training she stayed there and took them all, while Serenia watched with lips slightly parted and a small pink tongue flashing at the white teeth.

Cornelius was as solemn as ever, as if he took no pleasure in the sight but we knew for sure he did as the skin reddened and reddened, I saw his breath come faster in his breast, for he loved to see as well as to give. As I did. It was a steady measured birching, given with precision and with a sure touch and I knew I would dearly love to go to him myself one day for a repeat of the discipline, surely Cornelius would order it again!

And then Cornelius took Mary, lifted her in his arms, wiped away her tears, and rubbed the burning fine lines etched in whiteness over and over again until the red ran together to make one whole.

"Did you like that, my dear?" he asked, cradling her. She nodded, burying her face on his breast. "Now it is my turn for the gift" and he laid down before the fire on the thick rug, while we watched and said nothing.

How full his member was, how throbbing, how erect and firm! How lucky she was as we saw her legs part, her thighs widen to allow him entry, how his member cried one solitary tear before being pushed in with one fluid easy movement. Mary's head came back, her throat white in the firelight, her eyes pressed tight shut as she cried out under the sharp all consuming pain and then her eyes flicked open and were wide with wonder for his strokes were long and pure and hard, sure and steady and she must have felt it surge through her over and over again. His hands clutched and found her punished cheeks held them close, rubbed and pressed hard against the rug, reliving every stroke of the birching.

Cornelius came in a great rush, his buttocks heaving, his back wet with sweat from the fire and from his exertions. Mary lay still, a smile of pure contentment on her face.

And the church bells rang out the New Year.

We all had gifts in the end, for Serenia came to my bed with fingers and tongue, and to love the mound that is my and her brother's child.

And I have been promised a birching to end all birchings when the child is delivered safe and well into the world.

Would that it were soon!

I wish you every good wish for the New Year, dear sister, though I know not what you are doing, or where you are or what life is like for you now.

Would that I could post these letters to you!

CHAPTER 20
JANUARY 1970

Orders were orders, no matter where they cam form. These had come from Roger Grant himself, in a sealed envelope delivered by hand to the office.

"For Lauren Sanderson." The messenger handed the envelope to Linda who brought it across the office to Lauren. She put it down as casually as if it had been no more than another set of papers from Counsel.

"Love letters?" Stella, full of curiosity as always.

Liz had snorted with laughter. "For Lauren? She isn't interested in men!"

Lauren turned away. This was something she refused to share with anyone, even Judith. She corrected herself. That was a silly thought; if anything was going to happen at Roger Grant's place, it would happen with Judith's full knowledge and consent, as she was to be part of it. But the orders - Lauren hugged that secret to herself. And wondered whether it was because they were orders or whether it was because they had come from Roger Grant, or both.

The envelope moved from the desk to the drawer, from the drawer to her bag, as casually as if it were scrap paper she was taking upstairs. Lunch time seemed an impossibly long way away. Slowly the hands of the office clock dragged themselves around to 12.30. Lauren finished a letter, typed the envelope and dropped it into her out tray. Then she went to tap on Judith's door.

"I'm going upstairs for lunch."

"Fine." Judith, absorbed in a lengthy set of papers, hardly looked up. Lauren felt slightly disappointed, and then realised it wasn't a reflection on her, it was pressure of work. Sometimes it was hard to remember that.

Her flat as always was a peaceful corner of a busy world. If she listened hard she could just hear the sound of the typewriters, the bang of doors, the ringing of the shrill telephones and footsteps clicking along corridors, but in truth very little could be heard up here, away from everything. The cold January wind pressed against the windows, and she shivered.

The kettle hummed to itself as it heated up. Lauren buttered bread and spread honey onto it, not wanting much, wanting desperately to open the envelope, to find out what was going to happen.

Holding back was as much torment as reading it.

Finally, with a cup of tea on the small table at her side, Lauren carefully opened the large envelope.

Two photographs fell out, one of a bottom so marked that not an inch of white skin was left, the other a shy looking girl Lauren didn't recognise, wearing a high necked long sleeved black dress and high heeled shoes and standing in a submissive pose, eyes down, hands clasped before her, feet slightly apart.

Lauren gazed at the photographs for a long time, feeling wave after wave of emotion sweep through her, fear, anticipation, longing, a touch of being scared at the thought of the time it had taken to inflict those weals. What HAD inflicted those weals? Tawse, cane, strap? Then with a sudden and startling gasp she orgasmed right there, sitting in a chair, everything in place, not so much as the touch of vibrator or hand to make it happen, just the thought of what had happened to the girl with the black dress.

Lauren balanced the photographs on the arms of the chair, tried to control her breathing and her colour, sipped tea and stared at the girl.

One photograph was obviously taken after the other, wasn't it? Was this what was to happen to her? What was stopping her reading the papers which came with the photographs?

Nothing, she decided, feeling her heart rate return to normal, feeling the throbbing muscles quieten down, nothing but my wish to spin this out for a while. For my pleasure. If I read too much I'll not be able to work this afternoon!

And then wondered if it was right, whether she should have pleasure out of the whole thing.

Why not? It is my body after all!

Lauren spun round in shock. It had felt as if the words had been spoken aloud by someone who had crept into her flat unannounced, unnoticed, unheard. There was no one there. Nothing moved, not even a shadow, there was nothing but the rain now splashing against the windows, nothing but the enigmatic almost saucy smile of the girl in the green suit.

Lauren stood up, walked over to the portrait and looked up at the girl.

"Who are you?" she asked, feeling slightly silly at talking aloud, but realising no one could hear anyway. "Who are you? Why does your portrait look right here, why do I feel it was you I was waiting for? And didn't know it until Judith came in with the painting!" She stood back and watched as the changing light cast shadows over the girl's face, as if her expression was altering with Lauren's words. Now she looked mysterious, almost secretive.

"Whatever the reason, I know you belong here. You may have experienced the kind of love life I have, perhaps you even lived here!" Lauren laughed. "What a foolish thought! Life doesn't throw up coincidences like that, not even in fiction could I get away with that kind of coincidence! Listen to me - "

She sobered suddenly, glanced at the clock on the mantel and went to pick up her bag.

"Listen to me, turning sentences back on themselves for nothing. Well, whoever you are, you no doubt had a pretty name to go with the pretty face. You no doubt saw things I've yet to see, and lived a life I could not fully understand. All I do know is - you belong here, as much as I do. And I think you're going to be here for a long long time."

She hurried to the door. It was time to get back to work, yet she found herself listening hard for the sound of a whisper of a ghost living in her flat. There was nothing but rain.

"So, what's in the envelope?" asked Judith as Lauren moved around the little kitchen, making tea, preparing a quick meal of eggs and bacon for her mistress and boss.

"I don't know yet. I only looked at the photographs."

"Oh? Let me see." Judith went back to the lounge and picked up the solid brown envelope. Lauren followed her, wanting to see her reaction. The photographs slid out into Judith's hand and she looked at them, expressions chasing across her face, desire paramount.

"Gosh, this girl had one hell of a punishment! Is that what they have planned for you?"

Even as the words were said, Lauren felt the waves of emotion, felt it surge over her again, the mix of fear and lust, the odd quaking feeling in the pit of the stomach that was both pleasurable and painful at the same time.

"I imagine so." She went back into the kitchen, holding on to a worktop with both hands, wondering if she would be strong enough to take it, knowing that she would.

Judith followed her back there, listening to the spitting eggs and the sizzle of the bacon with an appreciative look.

"You've got to go buy identical clothes to the ones the girl is wearing," she told Lauren, waving the paper in the air. "Here's all the instructions. That gives you something to do, something to think about while you're waiting for the date to come around."

"When is it?" Lauren tried to keep her voice light, but the words came out as a croak, revealing the depth of her emotion.

"February 1st."

"Less than a month." Said calmly, but with a trembling that swept through her body, making her sit down suddenly. "I don't know what to think!"

"Enjoy it!" Judith put her arms around Lauren's shoulders, held her close, felt her trembling. "Enjoy it all, the anticipation, the shopping, the fantasising, and you'll do a lot of that! Because normally you only get this kind of chance once. I have heard it said if they like you they may want to do it again, but that will be entirely up to them. And you! You can say no! For now, concentrate on this one, and have a really good time. You're a natural submissive, you'll love it, all of it, before, during and after!"

"You've been to one already, haven't you?" Lauren lifted the food on to plates, set them on the table, pushed bread and butter toward Judith, who picked up her knife and fork eagerly.

"I'm starving! Yes, I have, when we've had this I'll tell you all about it."

With plates and frying pan washed and put away, with cups of tea and only one table lamp and the glow from the mock coal of the electric fire to light them, Judith stretched out her legs and looked at Lauren with eyes which glittered in the subdued light with a life of their own.

"I went to one of Roger Grant's trials last year. The girl was one Roger had found, I'd never seen her before, shy little thing, you can see that in the photograph. That's her - " she pointed to the letter on the coffee table. "They took her photographs as they do with everyone who comes, apparently, for the records. They chose to send you that one because she is most like you. Some of the others apparently have been brash outrageous young ladies who needed bringing down a peg or two in any event. A trial and the subsequent sentence usually does that.

"Some of the Bar's top ranking QCs were there, and I recognised at least one senior Civil Servant. Not that we make much play of recognising people, we're all there for the same thing, and we don't exchange much in the way of pleasantries. It's all comparatively informal in that Roger doesn't set out a room like a courtroom and yet somehow you know only too well someone is on trial, for their skin more than anything! I was an onlooker then, just one of the invited guests.

"At exactly 8 o'clock, literally as the clock chimed the hour, the girl walked in. She was wearing a high necked long sleeved black dress, black seamed stockings, black high heeled shoes, very plain, with a 3" heel. You've been asked to buy just that outfit. Well, she didn't speak, just stood, hands clasped in front of her, much as you stand. And waited. Roger approached her, told her she had been accused of witchcraft and had she anything to say in her defence?

"She shook her head and the trial began, with prosecution making the most outrageous claims that she had been seen with a familiar, etc. and the spells she had cast. Several men came forward to say they had been put under a spell by her. It was all over in a comparatively short time, and sentence passed: 'to be severely punished'. Someone brought in a large stool, with straps for wrists and ankles, and she was bound over it. Her clothes were shifted out of the way, a smooth white bottom appeared, small, rounded, rather like yours.

"I don't know whose slave she was, I didn't know then, I don't know now, what I do know is she was remarkably well trained and could take an awful lot. All of this had no doubt been agreed beforehand, so when someone stepped forward with a heavy tawse and started tawsing her, there didn't seem to be any cry of surprise or startled exclamations from her, she just took it.

"The tawsing went on for ages, hard, steady, with not a moment in between which is why I think she was well trained. It hurts so much to take it like that, without a second to absorb the pain. She was crying, steadily, but not sobbing heartbroken or anything like that, she was not in that much distress, or I think they would have stopped. You were wondering what caused those weals, weren't you? It was the tawse and then a small dressage whip, laid on over and over again. Then she did react, did cry out, did begin to show distress. But she never fought the bonds, never asked for mercy.

"Some women fantasise about being thrashed in public. I don't think you're one of them. She was, it showed, she was wet between the legs when they let her up. I know, because I had the chance to touch, to feel, to bring her to orgasm. I'll never forget the way her lips were wet with her flickering tongue and how she reacted to my fingers, muscles twitching and clenching against my touch. Her fantasy, to be thrashed in front of others, had been realised. Our fantasy, to have someone who could take heavy punishment, also realised. We all experienced a lot of pleasure that night."

Lauren considered. "It will be hard for me, not wanting to be seen by everyone."

"Of course. It's a test of obedience as much as anything! And an added thrill, to know you are submitting to my will, even though it goes against your nature. It's all part of it, my dear Lauren, do you understand that?"

"Yes, I do. You seemed surprised when Roger asked to borrow me."

"I was. At the time he hadn't seemed to enjoy his shy young girl, but I suppose he had, later, when he thought about it. He certainly enjoyed your visit, because he told me so. I used to think his tastes were mostly the louder women, those who came cocky and self assured, thinking they were capable of taking what was given and often were, but mostly they came for the money Roger offered, Money, yes, they got paid well, but they also had, to some degree, to enjoy it or it didn't work. People who don't like s/m show it by their immediate reaction to the pain, they start screaming for real and that would never do! Then he asked to see you, and I remembered this girl, and thought - well, yes, perhaps he would enjoy the quiet ones too, provided they showed they were really into all this, that they would get pleasure from the whole scenario and from the punishment."

"I'm afraid." Lauren twisted her hands together in her lap, overcome with shyness suddenly at the thought of it all.

Judith laughed. "Don't be afraid. Go along with it, just as you have with everything I've given you up to now. You'll love it. The main thing is - obey orders. At all times. There's satisfaction in just doing that, isn't there?"

Lauren looked up.

"You obey orders too, don't you? Your orders were to get me there. And you did it!"

Judith smiled, a little self consciously. "Yes, you're right. I'm a dominant in everything, except when it comes to a stronger man, then I give way just as you do! We're all the same, us women, giving way to the men in our lives."

"Do you - I mean have you - "

"Roger and I? Never. He's too proud a man to resort to such things as that, I don't know what he does for relief! I don't ask, I just accept he is superior to me!

CHAPTER 21
JANUARY 1870

My dear Sister,

We have had such a time here as you would not believe! It would be hard for me to tell you how excited we all are, and how Serenia and Cornelius have fussed and worried over me, insisting that the excitement is too much, and here I am, just four months into my pregnancy with five long months still to go!

The heart of all this is the fact that Mary and Briggs have been married this very day right here in the church of St Bridget!

Mary told me, in a quiet voice as we sat with our chocolate in my room, huddled before a fire leaping high in the chimney, creating sparks and patterns of red and the soot, that she had long feared that losing her maidenhead would mean no man would want her. But Briggs, or Louis for that is his name, a fine name for a surly man! had seen who had taken it, had known she came pure and clean to the touch of his Master, that she loved the sting of the strap even as he loved to give it and all in all there could not be finer wife for him. And a husband for her! But for me it means sadness for Mary is to leave my home and go to the country home of Cornelius and Serenia to be with her husband. And of course it is right for her to do so.

We had one week, Mary and I, one week to find a new servant for the house. Mary walked the streets as I had to find her, for I insisted we find another beggar, someone who needed a home, not just someone discontented with their lot in another house, for how long before they became discontented with this relatively solitary life?

We found one, together as it turned out. We were walking together along the Strand when a small girl approached us, a girl with shining gold hair and bright smile for all that she was dirty and probably ridden with lice. I left Mary to talk to her, to find out her secret, to find out she was runaway even as Mary had been. Before long little Ruth was installed in our household, cleaned and tidied and shown how to carry out the duties. I believe she will be a fine servant, and am waiting now for Serenia to order me to bring her under the discipline that all must live by who live in the house. For now it is enough that she is here and ready to work. Time enough for the discipline later.

For first we had to have the wedding. Alfred came from his newly rented home not so far from here, the other end of the Strand, where he lives in comparative poverty with his housekeeper/cook and one male servant, all that is left of his fine home and inheritance. How he has come down in the world!

Mary had a fine new blue dress, the finest the shop could provide for I said money was no bar to what she wanted, and Briggs had a new fine coat and breeches, not to mention high buttoned boots. For once a smile touched his surly face, for once I could see what a woman would see in him, for he is a fine set up man for sure. Little Ruth, for such is the way I think of her, had a new brown wool dress and lace collar, and looked as pleased and excited as if it were she who was to be married and not Mary! The Church rang with the sounds of our voices, and theirs, devoting their lives to one another, and Serenia hugged me for sheer joy. So much does she like to see her friends and workers happy!

Afterwards we came here for drinks and small sweetmeats, for much laughter and hugging and kissing all round. Louis Briggs stood afore the fire, tall and dark and smiling at Mary every time she glanced his way. Alfred seemed quite overcome at being asked to attend the wedding, at being such an honoured guest despite his new poverty, and sobbed into a handkerchief during all the appropriate moments.

As I anticipated, Serenia told me to bring Little Ruth under discipline as soon as possible. Cornelius held me close and whispered that the time could not go fast enough before I would be strapped myself, hard and long, to make up for the long periods of abstinence, but even as he held me and even as I protested I could not wait the child kicked against the wall of my womb for the very first time and we both felt it.

"There is your reason to wait," he told me, dark eyes aglow. And of course I will wait. I want this child as much as he, for I believe in my heart of hearts there will be more reward to come. Much as I love Cornelius and Serenia, I must still look to my future for at any time, as with Alfred, it could all fall apart.

Ah my sister, tonight with the sound of the wedding still ringing in my ears, for all that it is gone, the wheels of the carriage have crunched away over gravel and stone, taking Mary and Briggs, Cornelius and Serenia back to the country, for all that little Ruth is right now scrubbing and cleaning the many plates we seem to have used, and carefully washing the crystal glasses and I am here, in my room, sitting close to a fire for the January wind is cold and the rain harsh against the windows.

I must put away all thoughts of candles from now on, for the child could be harmed, and I know he is alive and well and kicking his way to strength and health and will come lively into this world. I must wait, perhaps indulge myself with a finger in the right place instead, for the thought of Mary and Briggs together in a bed tonight has thrilled me, the thought of what he might do to her white cheeks is filling my imagination.

And I feel a large amount of jealousy for all that she is a servant. For she is married and I am alone.

CHAPTER 22

Lauren hurried around the West End shops, looking for the right things in the January sales, hoping not to have to spend a fortune and touch the savings which were steadily building up in her account. They were her security, her defence against an uncertain future, for who knew when the tide of luck might turn again? Despite the rent and overheads, Lauren's bank account was slowly growing. No car to maintain and insure, along with no fares to worry about had made all the difference. There were the occasional gifts from Judith and the sizeable cheque she had received from Roger Grant for her visit. That had made her feel bad for a while, but she had banked the cheque and the thoughts had settled down.

In Saxone she found the right shoes, plain black court shoes, heel measured with a small ruler she held in her hand, yes, 3" heel.

"Do you have the other one to this?" she said, holding out the shoe to a small shy assistant. She could have been the double of the slave she had seen in the photograph.

There was another shoe, they fitted as if made for her. Lauren handed over the cash and hurried out of the shop with her carrier bag, desperate now to find the black dress that completed the outfit. The stockings were easy, the dress might not be.

But she found it, in a sale at half price and only needing the merest few stitches in a seam where it had come undone. When she got back to her flat, the phone was ringing. She dashed inside and picked it up, almost breathless.

"Lauren, this is Roger Grant. I've something to ask you, would you mind if I came over?"

"Of course not."

"Good. Give me half an hour, you know how hard it is sometimes to find a cab on a Saturday."

The line went dead and Lauren replaced the receiver, wondering what he could possible want. Then she shook her head. Of course he wanted to talk about the forthcoming trial! But why come when she could be summonsed there?

Half an hour was little time to put away her purchases, to make sure a duster had at least looked at the main furniture in the room, that the carpet was relatively clean and -

She combed her long auburn hair, letting it fall into waves around her shoulders. She changed into a plain black skirt and pale blue sweater, hung a silver pendant around her neck and added long drop earrings. She was surveying herself in the mirror when there was a tap at the door.

"Roger, do come in." She was flushed, wondering if she should be so casual and familiar, but he had used her first name over the phone.

"Thank you. I do hope I've not put you out by coming here?"

"Not at all. In fact, I'd just got home from completing my purchases, as ordered."

"Good." He sat down, looked at her with his dark eyes, and Lauren felt herself melting under his gaze.

"Was there - something else, something you wanted to add to the orders?"

"No, I came to ask you something else entirely. Since you came to my home I've not been able to get you out of my mind. Stupid, isn't it?"

Lauren looked down, said nothing but felt a huge leap of joy so intense it almost choked her.

"I've come with a proposition for you. I know you and Judith are - well, lovers. I also believe you would not be adverse to man in your life, am I right?"

"Yes." She continued to look down, afraid of what he was going to say, afraid he wouldn't say it.

"I'd like to think I could become that man. But to give you time, and space, and independence, I want to offer this. I'll buy this flat for you, and put it in your name. And we can - well, court one another, if you like, get to know one another properly. Then, if it works out, and we are to be married at some point, you can decide where you'd like to live, here, or at my place. If you decide to live with me, then this place could be rented and you could have the income."

Joy and happiness swept through Lauren, stilling her words. It was as if a dam had been breached. After years of struggling with her emotions, with dud relationships, with the sadness of departing partners, she was being offered a lifeline to money and security, to a possible life of happiness. For deep down inside she acknowledged that while she loved Judith she was also overwhelmingly attracted to this dark handsome man with his superior air.

"Judith is not a threat to me," he continued, as if he had read her thoughts. "For she is not a male. It is possible for someone to be bisexual, you know, and I would never reveal your secret."

"Could you - give me time to make up my mind?"

"No." He smiled as he said it. "I need to know for I am in a turmoil of feeling that will not settle, and that is not good for a barrister!"

"Then I accept immediately. I only asked for time because I did not wish to appear grasping and greedy."

"My dear Lauren, I am sure that would never be part of your nature!" He stood up, held out his arms to her and she went into his embrace for the first time. It felt right.

"Thank you," she whispered, as he kissed her.

CHAPTER 23

My dear Sister,

Would you believe what has happened in the last two weeks?

Of course not, for I have not set pen to paper to tell you!

Cornelius has been approached by a local squire and offered a considerable fortune by way of dowry if he would marry the squire's spinster daughter.

Serenia told me this over chocolate, much as Mary and I used to sit together to share confidences in my room. I felt shards of jealousy shoot through me, so hard I believed the child would suffer. Serenia saw it and held my hands tightly.

"He loves you, Clarisse, but we have a position to maintain, you know how it is! And we need money to take care of our estate and this home! But Cornelius has this to offer in its place. Now, be free to disagree or refuse but we think, that is Cornelius and I have talked this over at length, my dear Clarisse, at length! that this is for the best for all. We suggest you marry Alfred Lymardson for the child to have his name. Alfred can come and live here, in a house which will be put into a trust in your name, so Alfred cannot gamble it away from you. It means the house will be forever yours, and there will be a sum of money to help you maintain it, again in a way Alfred cannot touch. We do believe he is cured of his gambling but with money to hand, he may well begin again, so it is best to be sure. Now, my dear, what do you say?"

And I said yes, for two reasons. One is I owe dear Alfred a great debt, without him I could have been on the streets like Mary within days of arriving in this great city and two, I can face Papa as a married woman in her own right, with her own property.

"How does Alfred feel about this?" I asked, for surely they had approached him!

Serenia smiled. "Alfred is much taken with the idea, for it would fend off the comments that he - does not like women. Imagine him approaching the altar with a woman clearly in a certain condition! It would help his reputation abroad in the dining rooms of London and his club where he does so love to be! And he has long wanted a child too. For all that it is not his, it does not matter, it will carry his name."

All the arrangements have been made. Alfred came and we discussed it freely, because there are to be great changes. Alfred will bring staff with him. So our home is to be changed around. All the little rooms where I have lived for so long are to be turned over to the staff, Alfred and I will occupy Serenia's suite of rooms, and Serenia and Cornelius will come separately to London and use Cornelius's rooms, which Serenia will no doubt adapt for her own liking, I know she cares little for leather and old maps!

I have asked for just one concession, that a small room is set aside for me to keep for myself, where I can be alone to read my Bible and my John Bunyan, and other books I have discovered to be balm for my mind, and where I can write to you. Oh God send the day I can send these letters to you!

We hurried here and there to buy a suitable dress, I chose green, the same green as my beloved riding suit I am now too big to wear! and a hat with gold plumes and kid gloves that fit me like skin. High buttoned boots and a frilled parasol, I shall be the perfect lady to stand with Alfred Lymardson!

And so, dear sister, I am to be married even as Mary was in the Church of St Bridget here in London, and become a lady with a name. The wedding is tomorrow, I have one more night as a spinster with an illegitimate child in my womb. Tomorrow I will be respectable.

Let Papa do his will after that!

CHAPTER 24

Life suddenly took on a whole new happiness. Lauren was surrounded by love, she either spent her evenings in her flat with Judith as her companion or went to Roger's elegant West End home, there to be pampered and loved, for she had to remain unmarked for her 'trial'.

Urged by both Judith and Roger, she took a week's winter holiday and flew to Spain to spend time with her parents, 'away from temptation' as Roger put it, away from the temptation of his nearness. They had determined to stay no more than friends until the 1stFebruary had come and gone for fear it would influence the way Roger conducted the trial, or the way he handed out the punishment, if indeed it fell to him to do it. "I'll try and arrange for it to be me," he said, with a smile and a deeply loving kiss. "Now, go to Spain, and tell your parents all about the fine barrister you're going around with!"

She came back to even more snide comments with a hint of jealousy too. Reeves Marmon had been given the conveyancing of the flat, Mr Hazelton handling the transaction, Stella typing the papers. As Lauren talked back in on the Monday morning, glowing with Spanish winter sun, Stella had been full of spite.

"How did you get him then?" was the first question fired over the top of the typewriter.

Lauren shrugged.

"You know what it's like, you meet people at Court - "

"No, I don't know what it's like, I don't get to meet anyone stuck in this job!"

"There's plenty of other jobs," Liz observed, smiling at Lauren. "If it works out you're one hell of a lucky person."

"Thanks." Lauren ducked her head, embarrassed at their comments, not wanting attention drawn to her.

"It's all that toadying to the boss, that's what's done it!" remarked Stella, snatching papers out of her machine.

"Don't be silly." Liz gave her a 'shut up or else' look. "How could Lauren making coffee for her boss influence a meeting with Roger Grant?"

"Anything could happen when you live upstairs."

"Oh yes, people are trooping up four flights of stairs every day to see me!" snapped Lauren, but not meaning it. She felt too good for Stella to worry her.

But the news had obviously spread. During the morning various Solicitors and partners dropped by her desk, offering congratulations.

"Premature," remarked Lauren with a smile, showing a ringless left hand, but it didn't seem to deter them. All that mattered was one of their secretaries had ensnared the feelings, had attracted the attentions of a leading barrister, and it was good for the firm.

"All right if I take a surveyor up to the flat, Miss Lauren?" Mr Williams, looking worried, peering round the door.

"Fine by me. I think it's tidy!" Lauren smiled at him, and turned back to Linda, who was standing staring at her. "Needed for the mortgage," Lauren shrugged, trying to pass it off.

Linda went on staring. "So much attention," she breathed at last, with a wondering look.

"Not really. It's just that the purchase is going through right now, that's all."

And won't I be glad when it's done? she asked herself silently, looking at Stella's prim line of a mouth and disapproving scowl.

Later that evening, having dinner with Roger in a West End restaurant, Lauren confessed some of her doubts.

"I feel - out of my depth." She twisted a fork round and round in her hand, feeling her appetite slipping away from her. He was so handsome, so strong, so elegant in evening clothes it was almost unreal. It couldn't be happening to her, not Lauren Sanderson, the girl from Essex who had no real aspirations except to earn a living, virtually engaged to an eligible bachelor, someone with money and a glittering career ahead of him. To keep up with the social occasions she would no doubt need an entire wardrobe of small black dresses, heeled shoes, and a permanent arrangement with a hairdresser.

He smiled at her and once again she melted, as she did when Judith smiled at her in a certain loving way.

"My dear girl, forget your worries. You'll be fine. All I ask is that you be yourself, your own delightful easy going amenable self. That's all. There's no need to be special, to be outstanding. I love you because of what you are, a delight to my eyes and a balm for my ears. And you know how I feel about women usually! You're pretty special. Just keep hold of that."

The waiter removed plates and cutlery, stood waiting politely to see if they wanted anything else at that moment. Roger waved him away.

"We'll order dessert in a moment." He turned back to Lauren. "Someone's bothering you, aren't they?"

"Mr Hazelton's secretary mostly, she keeps making jibes, and it hurts sometimes, because I think she can see something in me, some weakness, something I lack, no one else can."

"No, she doesn't. I know about Miss Stella, Judith's told me. Ignore her. You're mine. All right?"

Lauren nodded, slightly reassured. If he knew about Stella then he could perhaps begin to realise how she felt.

"I think we'll choose the engagement ring right after the trial, so everyone will know it's for real. Does that suit you?"

"Yes." Lauren smiled at him, trying to control the sweep of feeling that went through her every time the trial was mentioned. It was coming closer all the time, and her anticipation grew with every passing day. She tried to distract herself with another subject.

"When will you have time to come to Spain with me to meet my parents?"

"Easter." It was said without hesitation. "We'll go at Easter, and we can spend time with them, getting to know them better. How does that sound?"

"It sounds wonderful."

Roger beckoned the waiter over. "We'll choose dessert now."

Back at his home, Roger sought to boost her confidence level further.

"The people you will be meeting, on the whole, will be people I have known for some time, who have helped me in my career, but most of all who share my inclinations. You'll find out at the trial just how many high ranking people are into this scene, my love! And all I have to do is to present you as my fianc'e and my slave. They'll accept that, and accept you, without question."

In that role Lauren knew she could be comfortable. To obey Roger in all things, to be subject to his slightest whim, yes, that was something she could handle, and delight in doing it.

"Then there's my parents, we'll invite them for dinner soon." He kissed her, holding her close to him in his strong arms. "Time's slipping by us fast," he told her in a whisper. "The trial is coming!" The usual shock of feeling followed his statement.

"I know."

"Once that's over, and you're truly initiated, everything will be fine. You're happy to marry me, aren't you?"

She nodded. "Of course."

"Not just because you're my slave?"

"I'm not your slave - yet."

"No, you're not. You came to me to obey Judith, not me." He frowned, pretending a severity he obviously didn't feel. "Well, that's something that will have to change." He snapped his fingers. "That will give a new element to the trial. I'll make it clear to everyone that it is your initiation to becoming my slave. That will also clear the way for future social occasions, won't it?"

Lauren felt all her cares seeping away from her. She had done the right thing in agreeing to come to Roger in the first place, to obey Judith's orders and come, to meet this exciting man with his exciting body mind and ideas.

"And I'll give you some orders to obey in the meantime, to ensure you remember to whom you belong!" He paused, stared at her, then a small grin began to creep on to his lips, pulling them out of line. "You can start by telling Miss Stella whatever her name is that you are my personal slave."

"Roger!" Lauren protested, and then fell back, laughing. It would change the way Stella looked at her, it was exactly right.

"That's an order."

"And I'll obey." She knelt at his feet, held his hands in hers, looked up at him with adoring eyes.

"The trial can't come soon enough for me!"

"Nor me."

Lauren felt the strength of his hands, wondered how it was going to be living life as a slave, knew even as she thought it the role would suit her, she was temperamentally suited to giving up everything for the sake of one man, and one woman.

Life was going to be good.

CHAPTER 25

My dear Sister,

So I am married. Here resides Mrs Alfred Lymardson of 30 Fleet Street, London, here resides Mr Alfred Lymardson, a glowing happy man. Oh how red his face becomes when he looks at me, how loving his embrace! We are living together as content as two people could ever be anywhere. Alfred makes no demand on me, my body grows with the child, he has felt the kicking, and is as excited as if it were his very own.

Little Ruth has grown considerably under our care and attention, good food and plenty of sleep in a proper bed have changed her beyond all recognition. How sharp she can be! But this is soon put right with a dozen good strokes of the strap which hangs behind the kitchen door as a permanent reminder to her.

Little Ruth does not care for the strap, she is not one to come to discipline as did dear Mary, now safely married to Louis Briggs and living in the country! but she is obedient enough, stays in place for the punishment which I am determined to give her for her faults and her cheek. Serenia will be content with that, for all that Little Ruth does not enjoy it. She has Mary, after all! and I am looking for a maid to help to do the heavy work around the house, for now that we have a housekeeper, and butler here, the heavy cleaning comes hard for little Ruth to do alone. The housekeeper does not turn a hair when I chastise Ruth, sometimes even reporting misdemeanours to me herself! A fellow enthusiast, I do believe. Or certainly a believer in the disciplining of young ladies.

And my baby grows, Sophie, it grows. I have tried to remember all the old tales dear Mama and others have told, to determine the sex of this child, but I fear I shall have to wait until the birth.

It is hard for me to tell you how good it feels, to know I am legally married in the sight of Man and of God Himself, that the child will have his name, that there is a man to escort me and protect me. Alfred is content, he has a wife which has relieved his image in Society. We entertain quite a lot, afternoon soir'es when guests call for a game of cards, no money changes hands any more, I see to that! which keeps Alfred amused and content, for he is not a man to lose himself in reading, although he much admires having a wife who can read so well. I myself am reading Mr Dickens' books and quoting sections to Alfred so he in turn can appear erudite among his friends. We have a good relationship, and it could not have been better contrived for your sister.

I pray nightly that you too will find a good man, Sophie, if you have not already done so.

A man to wed you and bed you and beat you to keep you in line. A man for the day and a man for the night. A daytime friend and nighttime company. A prayer all women should keep above their beds and in their hearts!

CHAPTER 26
FEBRUARY 1970

Sunday the 1st arrived at long last. Lauren dragged herself from a tumbled twisted bed, bleary eyed with lack of sleep and almost worn out with anticipation. Roger and Judith hadn't exactly told her not to play with vibrators, so she had, knowing that they would probably disapprove but when the feeling was so intense, so overwhelming, she had to have some relief, or she would orgasm right there in front of everyone when the first stroke landed. Now, at 8 am, she felt worn out, and incapable of raising a single sexy thought.

Her orders for the day were quite specific. Lauren picked up the sheet of paper, which she already knew by heart, and read it through again.

1. Do not dress until the moment you dress to come to the trial.
2. Do not bathe until the moment you are ready to bathe before dressing to come to the trial.
3. Do not wear briefs. You are to be aware of your body at all times and its availability to our needs.
4. Do not indulge in spirits or an excess of caffeine or tea. At all times your senses must be pure and aware.
5. You are to read no pornographic literature, or touch any sex toy of any kind. You must come ready for what we give.
6. At 4 pm precisely you will bathe, at 4.30 you will dress with care.

7. At 5 pm precisely you will leave your flat and hail a cab to come to the address given.
8. You will not speak to anyone other than the cabbie, and then only give him the address. Be discreet, be meek, be ready to be tried for your crimes.

The phone rang, startling her. To answer it would mean disobeying an order, but she could listen if nothing else. She picked up the receiver, carefully.

"Darling. I know you're not allowed to speak, but listen." Roger, low and urgent and almost secretive. "I just wanted to say I love you and that I'll be loving every moment of tonight." The line went dead. The words cheered her, consoled her, she felt suddenly less alone, without appreciating she had actually felt bereft and lonely before the call. There was a resurgence of feeling as the sexual element of the whole thing swept through her again. Her thighs clung together, skin on skin. Her legs quivered with suppressed excitement.

It was going to be a long day.

CHAPTER 27
D ear Letter -

Habits die hard, and I have written to my sister for so long now it seems strange not to address a letter to her.

But I confess I have long used these 'letters' as a journal anyway, a way to set down my thoughts and feelings. So I will continue, at least for a while, but there is no longer need to address my sister, for joy of joys she is here with me!

Alfred, dear Alfred, this time refused permission for our going out around the streets to find a suitable beggar woman, and asked instead that we advertise in a respectable paper for a new servant.

So I did, carried my written advertisement with my name clearly on it as the return address, Mrs Alfred Lymardson, 30 Fleet street, London. Betook myself in a growler to the offices of the Exchange and Mart and handed it in, a respectable advertisement for a respectable servant for a respectable household.

Of all the people who wrote to apply for the position, my sister Sophie wrote!

Alfred of course was as delighted as I found myself to be, and she came, we hugged and kissed and cried on each other and passed on all the news. Sophie has joined our household, Serenia and

Cornelius are delighted in her prettiness, for she is prettier than ever and if it were not for the child which grows within me I would be sore troubled with jealousy! Alfred do make a lot of her, and she blushes and flusters when he speaks.

Such happiness is mine!

CHAPTER 28

As the small delicate carriage clock chimed the half hour, Lauren began to dress, smoothing the black stockings, adding the high heeled shoes which were still comfortable and elegant, something to be grateful for. So often shoes didn't feel the same when slipped on later.

Inconsequentially she remembered Stella's look when Lauren finally obeyed her order.

"I'm Roger Grant's love slave," she told Stella in response to another jibe, watching with satisfaction as the jaw dropped, the eyes widened with shock and for once Stella was left speechless.

Liz had laughed heartily. "There you are! All your comments about Lauren being - well, gay I think is the polite word, isn't it? and all the time she's been Roger Grant's love slave! Good for you, Lauren!"

Stella had merely picked up her earphones and got on with her work, too shocked to say anything.

Lauren had returned to her desk, feeling a strange glow of satisfaction, as if she had just had a thorough spanking in earnest, not for fun. The few times Judith had been annoyed with her over mislaid documents, an indiscretion over the phone, she had been spanked for real, and it was very different from the games they played.

Obeying one of Roger's orders, no matter how humiliating it had been to make the confession, had had the same result - satisfaction.

Obeying his orders now felt good too, a deep glowing feeling that filled every part of her. She had begun a bath at 4 pm precisely, having been knickerless and in a robe all day. Excitement had mounted as the hands of the clock had dragged themselves round, through a light lunch, through a restless afternoon of trying to read without anything holding her interest. Eventually Lauren had given up trying to read, and instead sat and stared at the portrait.

"Just who are you?" she asked, as the shadows chased across the girl's face, altering her eyes and her smile. "I feel I almost know you!"

The phone rang but she ignored it, no need now for Roger's whispered words of encouragement, no intention of doing anything but obeying her written orders.

As the hands crept toward 5 pm Lauren picked up her coat and bag and went out of the front door. Experience had told her how long it took to click down the flights of stairs and be on the pavement. She began walking down, a hand gliding down the worn wooden rail, a strange sensation overtaking her. It was as if she had long flowing skirts swirling around her legs, as if a plumed bonnet sat on her head, as if the curls were dancing around her face, as if - as if she wore a green velvet riding suit and was on her way to an assignation on Rotten Row!

The church clocks were tolling 5 as she stepped out on the pavement, herself, the imagery gone.

"Back to being a 1970's girl" she thought, as she waved her arm at a cab. It drew up at the kerb, Lauren gave the address and climbed in, feeling herself go pale, feeling the excitement churning in her stomach, wishing she were anywhere but -

No, I wish to be precisely where I am. Obeying orders of my own free will, going to my destiny of my own free will. I wish only it were to be more private, this initiation. I dread being seen by others, for fear of making such a fool of myself.

Sunday traffic was light. The cab weaved and threaded its way through the cars and buses, past the occasional heavy lorry and jostled for road space with many black cabs.

Lauren had a key to Roger's home, but on this occasion she rang the door bell. It felt right. The door was opened by Roger, who told her by his expression she had indeed done the right thing. He gathered her into his arms and kissed her gently.

"I had the surveyor's report this morning," he told her, as she hung up her coat and bag. "He's only put one proviso in, that we get the bathroom wall attended to, the one with the damp? Apart from that, the mortgage is going ahead, so the conveyancing can too. It will soon be yours, my darling!"

"I'm so glad." But Lauren was white with tension, and not quite able to take it all in. Roger smiled sympathetically at her.

"For me. This is for me. Remember that."

Lauren waited patiently while he locked and then bolted the front door firmly. Obviously she was the last to arrive, no one else was being allowed in.

"Ready?" Lauren touched her hair, tugged her dress and checked her seams before following him to the huge lounge she knew so well, to find it full of people. A quick glance showed her many faces she recognised from television and newspapers, high ranking politicians, a few barristers, a Judge, Civil Servants. Some strangers were among them, but the majority she knew. Roger was right, he did have influential friends.

A hush fell over the gathering as she walked in. Every face turned toward her, expressions ranging from curiosity through admiration to pure lust.

Roger held her arm.

"Gentlemen, my fianc'e."

A murmur ran round the room. Some looked surprised: they obviously hadn't known. Most, however, just looked pleased. Roger turned back to Lauren. "You obeyed every order. You didn't pick up the phone a second time, we almost caught you out the first time though, didn't we?"

Lauren smiled, afraid to speak for fear everyone would hear the quavering in her voice. She was shaking inside.

Roger led her to the centre of the room, where a large padded stool waited. Lauren felt the pit of her stomach fall as she looked at it, appreciating what it was for. No straps. she had to do this of her own free will.

"Gentlemen, the defendant has arrived."

"Roger, old chap, who's going to prosecute?" The Judge was moving forward, smiling at Lauren.

"I thought I'd ask Percy." Roger indicated a stately elderly gentleman, the epitome of the English nobleman in Lauren's eyes.

"And the defence?"

"Why none other than my good friend Armstrong-Ffoulkes."

There was a good deal of amusement rippling around the room. Lauren knew, as others did, the two were deadly if friendly competitors for the best work in the Chambers.

"Who gives the sentence?"

"I wanted it to be me." Roger said it with a hint of steel.

"Unfair!" shouted a voice. "You'll get the girl afterwards, and forever!"

"Hear hear!" rumbled around the room, subdued thunder.

"I know that," Roger conceded. "So I have decided it has to be someone else."

"Who?" chorused the gathered guests, all anxious that it should be them. Lauren felt small, almost insignificant, they were arguing over her as if she were some trifle, some bone thrown to the dogs. Then she realised that this was it, how a slave would be treated, as nothing. Get used to it, she told herself, stiffening her spine and holding up her head.

"Then the sentence must be given by - " Roger paused, holding out the moment, making them all come alert with anticipation and eagerness. "I think the honour goes to Hubert this time."

Disappointment showed, but equally a good deal of head nodding. Lauren realised it was a wise choice, a sensible choice, an influential man given an opportunity few had.

"For those who have lost out I have others coming later - " A cheer went up, subdued but noisy enough all the same. Roger smiled at them all. "Did you think I'd let you go home dissatisfied? This is the Grant trial, after all!"

Armstrong-Ffoulkes moved over to Lauren, smiled at her. "I'm defending you, dear girl. It won't be easy, mind, because you'll no doubt plead guilty anyway, when you hear the charge."

Lauren smiled tremulously, put a shaking hand on his arm. "Thank you," she whispered, and turned to look at the person charged with giving her the punishment. The man called Hubert was small, grey, had a friendly look and yet a powerful bearing, it was as if strength and power radiated from his relatively small frame. While others towered over him for physical height no one seemed to match him for physical presence. A wetness told Lauren she had come face to face with a true Master, and it would be something she would long remember.

"Shall we begin?" Roger gestured to his guests, getting them to sit or stand away from the centre of the room, clearing a space for the trial. I am not happy being on show, thought Lauren desperately, wishing she had something to hold on to.

Hubert walked over to her. "My dear." She looked at him firmly and squarely, without a hint of her inner quaking. "My dear, I will be hard on you but fair. To be given the task is an honour and I will long remember it. You are a fair maiden for our friend Grant here, I wish him every happiness, and you of course."

But Lauren felt she was an after thought.

She stood, hands clasped, head bowed, while a photograph was being taken. Then she held her head up, looked at them in turn, saw the looks read pure lust and felt her own excitement building to an impossible peak again. I WILL enjoy it, she told herself.

Percy came closer, a man with languid graceful movements, and a sharp mind few would beat. He held a piece of paper.

"The trial of Lauren Sanderson begins." A hush fell over the room, everyone stopped moving, or talking or rustling themselves in their chairs, "Lauren Sanderson, you stand accused of being hopelessly in love with Roger Grant. How plead you?"

"Guilty." A smile creased her lips. She might have known Roger would come up with something very silly like that!

Percy turned to the audience, a smile creasing his face in return.

"What is there to say, gentlemen, except that the prisoner here has pleaded guilty to a crime of caring. I ask you - " he threw his arms wide - "how can we deal with young ladies who so recklessly throw their emotions to the four winds in this manner? What has this Roger Grant done to permit the affections of such a impressionable and flighty young girl? Does she have the right to give her love to a fine upstanding member of the Bar?"

"Objection." Geoffrey Armstrong-Ffoulkes got to his feet, strolled over to Lauren, and put an arm around her waist. "This young woman - "

"Your turn will come later, Mr Armstrong-Ffoulkes." The Judge put on a severe look, while his eyes showed his amusement. "This is not an American court, we do not allow Objections to be shouted in that way. Mr Prosecutor?"

Percy bowed. "I rest my case, Your Honour. There is little more to say in prosecution, the fact is clear, love is writ in her face, and it is as clear as day to the rest of us that young Grant returns the affection, fool that he is!"

Geoffrey Armstrong-Ffoulkes rose again and looked round at everyone.

"Lauren Sanderson is young, sure she is, but with some experience of life, or so I hear tell. And Roger Grant has taken full advantage of that to twist and turn her affections for his own evil ends, he has encouraged and entrapped this innocent young girl into his wily arms, into his flat and into his life. She had no chance against such a scheming member of the Bar! And I am sure they are going to be gloriously happy together!"

"Guilty as charged." The Judge waved a hand at them all. "There is no defence to the charge of love, and no need to prosecute either."

"Sentence, Your Honour?" asked Percy with a malicious gleam in his eyes.

"Hubert knows how to give a good thrashing, to bring her to her senses."

"Or to show her what she can expect from the hands of her Master," added Roger, smiling encouragement at Lauren from across the room. Lauren blushed, wishing her heels weren't quite so high, they were beginning to make her feet ache. It was an incongruous thought at the moment when every man in the room was wishing they were in Hubert's position as he walked over to her, holding a wooden backed hairbrush. It was very like the one Lauren had bought on Judith's order and she knew what devastating results it had.

Hubert took her arm, led her to the stool and pushed her over it. With something close to a sigh Lauren settled herself, gripping the bar that held the legs together, feeling Hubert arrange her clothing, wishing she had worn briefs but following her order to the letter. A collective gasp ran round the room when they saw her unmarked flawless cheeks. She knew they were shapely, knew they were good to look at, and face down her blushes could be hidden. And yet underneath the blushes was a tiny glint of pleasure that she was good to look at, and the men were enjoying looking at her. It helped cover the deep embarrassment that swept over her, equalling in intensity the sexual feeling the whole trial had given her. Her stomach ached with the need for release, for pleasure, for a period of calm. It had been a long build up, the day had been long, the trial relatively long - or had it? It felt like a long time.

It felt even longer before the first sharp smack of the hairbrush found a cheek and she gasped, as much with shock and surprise as in pain. Again on the other cheek. Hubert was finding his stance, his rhythm. Lauren clung hard to the bar, knowing she dare not move. This is for Roger, she told herself over and over again as the hairbrush fell with relentless hardness, fire leaping through her, stinging pain followed by deep burning. The sound of the smack was instantly followed by another leap of pain.

"Are you counting?" asked Hubert in a deep voice of pure authority.

"No!" Lauren gasped in dismay, anticipating more punishment.

"It's all right, I didn't ask you to, but you've had ten on each cheek if you want to know." A long pause. Lauren allowed herself to relax, to unclench her hands, to feel rather than see the men staring at her, feel their collected lust filling the room with overpowering feeling of pure desire.

"A paddle!"

Hubert's voice was firm and sure, as were the strokes that followed.

The paddle was punched through with holes round the rim. each one bringing ridges, pin pricks of skin to the surface, it stung harder than anything else she had ever had. She cried out at every stroke, somewhere between a sob and a laugh. It was easy to forget the audience when so much pain was being given in so firm and steady a way.

"Stand up." Lauren pushed herself up, feeling herself rock on her heels, finding her balance, standing still.

"Skirt up." She tugged at the black dress, lifting it above her hips, knowing they were looking at her tangle of auburn hair, her bright red cheeks. She longed to rub, but holding the dress up stopped her touching herself, and they knew it too.

Everyone seemed frozen in a long long moment, it seemed to go on forever, until the order was given to lean over the stool again, and Hubert approached her, swinging a heavy tawse before her eyes.

"A tawse!"

Leather after leather, pain over pain. The tawse cut wide bands of pain where the paddle had raised round slabs of pain, the burning went deep, as did the feeling

'I am doing this for Roger.' She was delighting in being made to stay down, to take such a severe thrashing, to burn in front of so many men knowing she was giving them pleasure as well as her own lover.

No chance to breathe this time, no chance for the pain to subside, a cane cut a bright line across her and this time she did scream out with shock and surprise and pain. Her hands locked around the bar, Lauren desperately held on to the last of her will power to stay in place to take the caning, which cut every single time through the deep redness and into the deeper muscles for her cheeks, burning and cutting.

He aimed for the thighs, for the gentle soft curve of the cheek, for the high thinly covered part, everywhere, there was no escape the finely drawn lines of pure agony.

When he finally stopped she had no energy to get up, she just lay over the stool, helplessly sobbing. A spontaneous round of applause broke out, a camera clicked, the photos for the record were being taken. Then gentle hands reached for her, lifted her, kissed her tears. She opened her eyes, water running from them, saw Roger smiling at her, saw his concerned face, knew how much this meant to him, and tried to smile.

"It's all over."

Lauren stood up, clung to his arm, accepted the large handkerchief and dried her face. Hubert was standing in front of her, a look of admiration writ clear.

"You did remarkably well, young lady. I had thought to bring you to your feet long before I was done caning you."

"This was for Roger," she told him, leaning forward to kiss his cheek. He glowed with pleasure.

"Not often I get to deliver the sentence and get kissed afterwards." Hubert went to get a drink at the bar in the corner of the room, leaving Lauren and Roger clinging to one another.

"Now you're mine forever and ever," he told her.

"We'll buy the ring next week," she whispered, kissing him.

It was what she wanted. To be punished hard, to be brought to the very edge of giving up, and to take it. To be totally submissive to Roger's will, no matter what he asked, no matter what he told her to do.

In that moment an orgasm rippled through her and she clung to him, pleasure chasing across her face. He knew what had happened, smiled and kissed her.

"You'll find some knickers in the bedroom," he told her. "You might feel more comfortable wearing them."

Lauren slipped off the high heels, their job done, and padded across the carpet to the door.

Knickers would feel good, she told herself, ignoring the smiles and conversation gambits of the gathered men, making her way to the bedroom.

Where a surprise waited.

Judith was sitting on the bed.

CHAPTER 29
MARCH 1870

Dear Letter - it is a quiet night. The church clocks are chiming the hour and I should be resting, but tonight I feel restless and the child within me wants to move and turn. It is time to set down some thoughts and observations, mostly of what Sophie has told me of home.

The baby died, as I afeared she would: how I pray that mine may be well vigorous. Thomas is grown strong and hard, and is bound to follow Papa into the church. Mama is poorly, she says, from working too hard and being prayed over too much. Here we keep to the simple prayers, Grace before meals, a prayer on leaving the house for the wilder areas of the great city, a prayer at night for all we love, and church on Sunday.

Papa is as bad as ever, she says, which is why she answered the advertisement, to escape his constant wrath. For all that, Sophie has come to love the feel of the strap - but I have to state here I could not bring myself to punish my dear sister, to whom I feel so close and always have. No, it is not for me. Serenia has introduced Sophie to the joys of both the strap and Sappho, and Sophie has responded as I hoped and prayed she would. Indeed, Cornelius asked if there were more of us at home -

I do believe a romance will bloom between Sophie and Alfred's butler, for they are making eyes at one another all the time, and he is seen talking to her in the servants' quarters.

It is cold tonight, it has been a cold start to Spring. Tonight I am weary, and wish for this time to be over, I long for the touch of a man and a woman, for the pain which brings pleasure, for the release from aching need. Yet I have to say Cornelius is the most considerate of fathers, Alfred the most considerate of husbands, I the most fortunate of women!

For I sit here in a home I own, something few women can say. I have savings, for they continue to grow in my account, I have consideration and love all around me. I feel for the poor beggar women out on the streets, when I have more money I will do something for them, set up a trust, ask the church to distribute clothing and food for them, or something. Tonight my mind ranges over many things.

I will ask Alfred to take me to my home when I have given birth to this child and can find a nanny to take care of him, for I have a fancy that it shall be a lusty boy.

Then I will ask Alfred to take me to my home to confront the man who stands between me and total peace of mind. I wish to be reconciled to Papa and Mama, I wish to show him a wayward wilful daughter can become a woman of wealth and respectability in society. I will go with a husband on my arm and child at home, and a house in my name.

But now I close this journal. Ah my pretty letter, what more would you have me tell, what more could I desire, for now I am at peace and the future may take care for itself...

Chapter 30

"All right, Miss?"

The builder stood with his arms akimbo, surveying the small bathroom. "All right - we'll have a look see what's causing this damp for you. Pretty bad, ain't it?" He scratched thick thatch of unruly brown hair and grinned at her. He took a pouch from his pocket, began to roll a cigarette without looking at the nimble fingers.

"Do you think it's just condensation?" asked Lauren.

"If it was, the surveyor wouldn't't've said he didn't like it, nah, I think it's a touch more than that. Might be a leaking pipe somewhere round here - " He lit the cigarette, crouched down, began prodding the wall. "Here, it's not brick!"

"I know." Lauren looked at him in surprise. "Haven't you found wooden walls before?"

"Yeah, but not here, these buildings are all made of brick and stone!" He prodded harder, a gap appeared. "Hold on." He took up a chisel, pressed it against the wall, and banged it hard with a calloused hand. Lauren fleetingly wondered how such a hard hand would feel giving a spanking and dismissed the thought instantly.

Then reconsidered it. I can fantasise, can't I? She grinned secretively, and then her eyes widened in shock.

A large hole was appearing in her wall, and beyond it - a small room.

"Well, I be jiggered!"

Lauren pulled at the ancient wood, anxious to get inside this haven of Victorian splendour, anxious to see what her flat really contained.

"I've heard about this." The builder helped her pull the wood away, stacking it in the bath for convenience. "They partitioned some of these rooms, make smaller ones, usually there's a door, this time there ain't. Would you look at that?"

Lauren stepped over the partition and into history. A small table stood in the centre of the room, covered in a thick dusty fringed tablecloth. In the centre, a paraffin lamp, smutty glass and dried wick still showing. A high backed wooden chair tucked under the table, a thick rug still covered the floor. Samplers hung on the walls, religious texts, delicately traced names and dates. A small cabinet leaned against one wall, filled with papers and dried up ink. A Bible rested on top, well worn, well read. "You can get a dealer in here, give you a good price for this stuff," observed the builder, looking around in surprise. "Well well, who'd have thought it?"

"I'll keep all this," Lauren decided instantly. "If it doesn't fit here it'll fit well in my fianc"'s flat." She walked over to one of the samplers, dusted the glass and peered at it.

"Clarisse Lymardson. 1882.

That's me in the portrait. A voice in her ear, clear as if someone had spoken by her side. Lauren spun round, almost expecting to see the bright eyed girl in the green suit appear by the table. She looked round the room, smiled as thoughts and impressions rushed into her mind. She could see this Clarisse Lymardson, the curls dancing, the dark eyes full of mischief, sitting at this table, reading her Bible, thinking her thoughts ...

Writing her letters?

Yes, there were letters, bundles of them in the cabinet, old and yellowing.

"Well, what do we do with all this?" asked the builder, looking as surprised and as pleased as Lauren felt.

"I'll need to think about it." Lauren felt as if she was breathing History. "Can I call you?"

"'Course you can. All right, Miss, I'll have the rest of the day off, I don't mind!" He gestured to the bath full of splintered wood. "I'll get a lad up here tomorrow to get rid of that for you, will that be alright?"

"Yes, I can wait for a bath!"

The builder grinned, looking her up and down, a twinkle in his eye, but made no comment. He clomped his way out of the flat, Lauren at his heels. She closed the front door after him, and stood with her back to the panels, considering.

Lauren leaned against the door, a small smile touching her lips, a flutter of feelings rushing through her body. The look had been calculating, had said volumes if she cared to read volumes into it.

No way. With both Judith and Roger, she needed no other lovers, but in her mind she was free, free to soar on the wings of a fantasy as often and as much as she liked, it was one thing Roger had never stopped her from doing.

She sank into the armchair, looked up at the portrait, and smiled. "I bet you indulged in some fantasies during your time, just like I'm doing now!"

She leaned back, closed her eyes, let her mind wander -

The builder had hard calloused hands, used to ripping out wood, to pulling nails from planks, to hammering and -

"You've been bad," he told Lauren, who was standing before him, toe scraping the ground, the picture of a little girl who had done wrong. "Bad bad bad all through. There's only one cure for bad girls. Come here."

Walking closer, slow careful footsteps, wanting yet not wanting, pain is always feared yet longed for, anticipation churns, apprehension tingles, feelings flutter wildly and there is no going back. Ever.

Knees are hard, hands even harder, sharp stinging slaps on protected and unprotected cheeks, and briefs, no matter how flimsy how limited in their protection and covering, are pulled down out of the way. A grunt - of admiration or approval, or sheer energy, who can say? Lying still, feeling silly, feeling scared and yet sexy, she waits, knowing there is more, much more, to come.

The spanking starts.

The hand is as hard as a paddle, yet touched with warmth, then heat as it strikes over and over, she is wriggling, she is struggling, she is loving every single moment, every sharp stinging slap, every sensation which surges through her, every hint of wetness that touches her thighs.

Only when tears spurt unwillingly from her eyes does he stop, allowing her to fall to the ground, orders her to lie still, to let him look -

Lauren unwillingly opened her eyes. She had come close to a shattering orgasm, close to but not experienced, wasted ....

He hadn't been strong enough, that builder, he had been hard in her mind, but somehow, despite his look, he wasn't a man who would or could dominate. She got out of the chair, looked at the portrait, and reached for the telephone.

Things to be done. Roger to be told -

Yes, Roger needed to be told. Perhaps Judith too, surely she would be interested in the find. She had after all got the flat for Lauren.

And Mr Williams too, that dear little man with his old fashioned ways –

Lauren phoned him first, trying to explain the find without letting too much of her excitement show. He promised to come round the very next morning to see it.

Judith sensed Lauren's excitement, joining in with it. "I'll be right up!" she told Lauren. "This I must see!" Lauren replaced the phone, glad she had a few days' holiday in which to savour this discovery.

Then she phoned Roger, who was on the point of leaving Chambers.

"Listen, we had a tremendous find, she said, thrilled just to hear his voice on the phone, deeper and richer than it was in real life. Telephone lines distorted voices, often adding something in the distortion. "The builder found the wall was wood, and so damp we broke right through. There's a whole room on the other side, Roger, a room full of wonderful things, a table, a chair, carpet, samplers, a cabinet, complete with letters -"

"It sounds fascinating," he told her. "I'll be there as son as I can. Sorry, darling, I must rush. I love you."

"I love you, too."

Lauren replaced the receiver, and looked up at the portrait.

"You," she told the green suited girl, "you were a woman in love. It shows. I see that now. That look, that smile, that joy of life which only comes when you're in love. I'd move you into the room, where you belong, so you could look down on your table, your cabinet; but first, I don't think I can leave it like that; unlike you Victorians, I need a proper bathroom; and second, look at all the trouble Mr Williams had putting the hook up for me! You're altogether too heavy for me to move! But that's where you belong, in there, with the furniture. And the letters ..."

The letters!

They would give her an insight into this woman whose portrait had haunted her, whose presence had haunted her, from the moment she arrived at the front door. All right, she told herself, they'll be one sided, I won't know what she wrote, but I'll know what the people wrote back, won't I? She'd read them later, when she'd decided what to do, when the experience of having this surprise is absorbed and made part of my life. In the meantime -

Lauren fetched the letters, smoothed the beautiful paper, caught glimpses of a flowing copperplate hand, and stored them in her bedroom. They were to precious to be looked at by everyone. She might show them to Roger, later, but no one else was having a sight of her find.

Judith called out and Lauren hurried to let her in. They spent a happy hour together, exploring the find, exclaiming over the bible, and all the wonderful things in the room.

"I heard about this sort of thing once before," Judith said finally, when they were sitting with cups of tea huddled round the electric fire, for the day had turned out cold and damp. "Someone was doing up a bathroom and broke through a wall just like that, found all sorts of bills and invoices from an earlier age. It's very exciting! What are you going to do?"

"I don't know," Lauren confessed. "I'm waiting for Roger. The whole thing will need re-thinking now."

"Well, I have to go, there's work to be done and the temp isn't as fast as you. Hurry back, dear, I miss you." With a loving kiss, Judith left her alone.

Lauren returned to the shattered bathroom, and looked at herself in the small bathroom mirror on the way to the new room, wondering at her heightened flush, her sparkling eyes, wondering at her feeling that the letters were for her eyes only at first.

The room was less musty now it had been opened to the outside world for the first time in a great many years. Lauren stood on the dirty rug, where Clarisse's feet must have rested so many times, and stared at the wall, at the huge gaping hole which let in the subdued light that a frosted window gave.

Who had had this room blocked up, and why?

I'm standing in History!

It was a strange feeling, one that was hard to identify. Touching a bible which Clarisse had probably read: the pages marked where fingers had turned them many times - it was not a showpiece bible, for sure. Lauren pulled out the chair, sat down on the seat, put her legs under the table and rested her elbows on the thick cloth.

What were the Victorians like when it came to discipline?

Oh how prudish they were with their covered piano legs; tassels and covers for everything; long sweeping clothes to hide the ankles; no mention of 'goings on' or periods or pregnancy; a strange and outwardly virtuous lot. Everyone knew they were sexually active - but discipline? Where did that feature in their lives?

Rather prominently, she suspected.

She leaned back in the chair, hands on the cloth, wondering, thinking, letting her mind drift.

What if we were to use this room before it gets cleaned up and sanitised, what if we, Roger and I, were to come in here -

Oh, he would be proud and strong, wouldn't he, in a brocade waistcoat and full breeches, gold watch chain and curling whiskers, and I, subservient to him in a dark blue gown with lace collar, a small cap for my hair and my eyes modestly downcast.

"I asked you to come here because you are consistently failing in your duties." "Yes, Master." "What is the problem? Am I not giving you enough wages? Are you not having enough time off? Do I not give you one afternoon a month to yourself?"

"Yes, Master, you are very kind."

"So - why are you defaulting in your duties?"

"Master, I - " Trailing off, no real answer to the question, there is none, there is no real reason for it.

"I suggest some discipline may help correct your ways. Go fetch me a birch."

"Yes, Master."

With a quiver of fear and a touch of excitement I leave, hurrying to the kitchen where the birch stands in its pail of water, always ready.

The last time was on young Jack, the stable lad, who had allowed a horse out with a loose shoe which it cast in Hyde Park, nearly injuring a passer by and causing the horse to go lame for a few days. Then Master had taken Jack into the scullery, had put him over the scrubbing table and pulled down his breeches. With all the staff present to add to his humiliation, Master had given him twenty-four with the birch.

How Jack had howled and screamed for mercy and promised to do better but he took them all, all twenty-four of them. Word had it he ate his meals standing up for some time after that.

Now I am to be birched! I have no idea how it feels, I can only relate to what I saw; the fine thin strands biting into his white cheeks, red lines springing into full view, criss crossing a fine pattern of pain.

Cook watches me collecting the birch, says nothing, but Lizzy, the scullery maid, does.

"Getting your desserts, are you, Miss Hoity Toity? I do hope Master lays it on good and hard, and you knows how it feels to be standing up for meals for a few days!"

"Hush, Lizzy, hush your mouth, or Master will be after you with the birch!" Cook is anxious not to have dissent in her kitchen staff but Lizzy is not abashed. "Master could birch me all he pleased, fine man that he is, I'd be proud to drop my pantaloons for him!"

Higgins, the butler, comes into the kitchen. "Enough of that talk!" He sends Lizzy scurrying to the scullery to be out of the way. Higgins looks at me and, like Cook, says nothing. They all know Master is a man to punish, that it is his delight to punish, and that his excuse is just that, an excuse.

Back up the flights of stairs, a hand trailing along the wooden rail, hesitant yet anxious to get it over, apprehensive yet excited at the thought of what is to happen.

"You are long in coming!" he snaps, taking the birch from me. "Get over that table!"

The cloth is thick, the table edge hard for all that, digging into the bones that sit between the hips, those bones I caress at night, sliding a hand the length and softness of the skin, feeling the bush of hair tangling round the fingers, feeling the opening, the wetness, the sheer joy of touching myself, which is wrong, everyone knows it is wrong, and yet, who can say what is wrong in the darkness, when there is naught but the moonlight to see what fingers do and faces betray? For I touch myself and pretend it is Master.

Fingers are at the laces, at the ties, are fumbling with the bows and knots, are tugging the clothes away from me, are allowing the cold afternoon air to touch my skin. An indrawn breath, it is the first time Master has seen me, I am new here and I must please him.

But there is no time to consider the feeling; the first stroke has landed, its lacework of pain firing its way across my cheeks.

I squeal and he is angry.

"Stop that noise immediately! There are many more to come, and I cannot stand a woman screaming under discipline! Be silent or be gagged."

I bite my tongue and am silent: the next stroke falls, covering the original fine lacework with more. The tips of the birch catch my hip, cut into me, I am -

Wet.

Four strokes are given fast, no time to catch a breath, no time to absorb the pain. Now there are six strokes to take in, six burning sets of lines.

He lets me wait, leaning on the table, clutching the cloth with both hands, biting my lips, red of face and red of bottom cheeks displayed for him to see to touch to punish ...

"I think another six."

He begins again. It is worse now, for there has been time to absorb the last ones, but not for the burning to leave me, they hurt even more, were that possible!

Another six I am given, and have to wait while he considers his handiwork.

"Disobedience of your standard deserves severe punishment, do you not agree?"

I dare not speak, to agree may being further punishment!

"I said - " - the words are given with two more strokes - "Do you not deserve more punishment?"

It seems I will get it whether I speak or not.

"Yes, Master."

"Then you will take another dozen."

A dozen! And I do, but with shouts and squeals and cries for mercy and a burning that goes deeper than any I have had before; a feeling that the birch will break on me; that the pieces will fly everywhere; that the feeling it generates will explode in me -

"Enough."

It is enough. I could not take any more. But then again, if Master says I must have more then I will of course have to take it.

Then a thick and solid stiffness enters me, fills me, touches every nerve, brings the feeling to a peak of sheer ecstasy and I explode explode explode -

Lauren was brought out of her fantasy by a sharp rapping on her front door. She hurried to open it, aware she was very wet from the explosion of feeling she had just experienced, induced by the emotive atmosphere of the small room and its contents.

Roger was smiling, holding out a pretty wrapped box for her to take.

"To celebrate your find," he told her, after kissing her passionately.

Lauren opened her gift, finding a pretty Victorian posy pin nestling in a fluffy cloud of cotton wool. Before she could express her pleasure, he put a finger on her lips.

Not a word. I've not brought you much in the way of gifts, this is to make up for that."

"I don't need gifts, Roger!"

"Oh but you do! I should be showering you with gifts. Now show me this room."

He followed Lauren into the lounge and then through into the small now disrupted bathroom. For a few minutes he stood staring at the shattered wall, looking into the room with its treasures of Victorian furniture and the rug. Lauren stood patiently by, knowing how she felt when she first saw it, knowing he needed time to assimilate the discovery.

"It's magnificent!" He turned to Lauren. "But what do we do now? You need a proper bathroom and everything."

"I know. We need to talk about this."

"But before we do - " He turned back, stepped through the broken wall and into the still slightly musty room, touching the cabinet, running a hand over the cloth covered table, sitting on the high backed chair. "Before we do, we should act out a Victorian fantasy here. Tonight! Go find yourself a long blue dress, preferably one with a lace collar, and I'll go find myself an outfit - and a birch!"

Lauren's breath caught in her throat. How did he know, how could he know?

"And tomorrow we'll get an architect in to draw up fresh plans for the flat. This is going to cost us a lot of money, but I think it will be worth it."

"Roger, I - " Lauren started to tell him about her fantasy and stopped. It was a secret, one she should share with Clarisse and no one else. She changed the words. "Thank you so much, despite what you say about not thanking you, for the lovely pin."

"I'm glad you like it."

They went back to the lounge, where Roger looked up at the portrait. "It is her room, isn't it? No one else would feel so right in this place."

"I found some letters," Lauren began, tentatively, still not sure whether she wanted to talk about them. Something was holding her back, a premonition of what she would find written in that lovely copperplate hand? "I don't know what they will reveal yet about the lady in the painting, but yes I do think they are about her."

"Interesting. All of it is interesting stuff. You'll need to decide whether to keep the furniture - "

"Oh, I'm keeping it, all of it. Everything will fit in the flat; it suits the feel of the place, I can replace some of this which Judith got for me. It's nice, it fits well, but to have the original is far better."

"I agree. Change of subject; you like the idea of the fantasy for tonight?"

"Great idea. It will be fun, just once, to use the room as it was, not as it is going to be." She smiled, holding out her hands to him. "How long do I have to get changed?"

"Three hours."

"It isn't long."

"You need time to obey orders?" Roger stood, gathering her easily into his strong arms. "I'm so lucky to have found you!"

"And me to have found you too."

"I'll be back."

"Make it soon."

"Three hours. That's all you have."

"It's all the time I need; if you give the orders, I will obey."

The dress was soon converted from a ball gown, with the addition of a lace collar from an old blouse, the posy pin attached to her breast. Lauren curled up her long hair into a nest of ringlets, smoothed pale powder over her face and smiled at her reflection.

One hour to go before Roger came back, every inch the stern Victorian gentlemen she knew she would find on the doorstep.

One hour.

She got out the letters.

Just enough time to start to read ...

JULY 1869.

My dear Sister,

Sister, I have felt rage from Papa before, when I broke the fine china dish that was his mother's wedding present to him, when I did stand knee deep in the river ...

EPILOGUE
LONDON, 1971

Dear Clarisse,
   This feels strange. For someone so used to typewriter keys, to all that modern technology has given us, to sit here with a pen, to write to you with a real pen and real ink is very strange.

But only a pen and ink will do, as it is the only thing which will fit with your letters. I have bought unlined paper, and a fine pen, with dark blue ink to match yours.

I should start by explaining I have your letters, all of them, and very revealing they are too.

It is very fanciful of me to want to sit and write to you after reading your letters, but I feel I want to put my thoughts down, even as you did. And after all, I do sense your presence around me, particularly when I use your furniture.

To start at the beginning: we, that is, the builder and I, found your room. Roger and I decided what to do with it. After much discussion, the room was finally converted into a large bathroom, with all mod cons, so the flat could be better used. I hoped your letters would reveal why the room was blocked off, but there was no clue. Did Cornelius order it to be done, or Alfred? Did you die before him, so he couldn't bear to have your things around? There are many possibilities.

I will never know.

All your furniture, rug and samplers, were taken to Roger's house and put into what became my dressing room.

So I can say in truth you once sat writing to your sister at this table; even if it is not in the same place.

Your letters talked of love and fear and lust and passion. Even when your sister came to be with you, the letters carried on in the form of a Journal.

I know so much about you from reading your letters and from looking at your portrait.

What I've not done is tell you about my life - which is so much a copy of yours!- and finally I intend to put my letter, along with your many missives, in a safe deposit box in the vaults of Messrs Coutts & Co. I had thought to publish the letters, but now I know they are too personal, too close to what we - you and I - have experienced - to share with the world. Yet.

Let me truly start at the beginning.

Roger and I were married in St Brides Church, which you knew as St Brigid's. I wore the conventional white silk flowing gown, veil smothered in tiny seed pearls, page boys to hold my train from the ground. Afterwards we had a splendid and very expensive reception in a huge hall in Cheapside. Everyone said I looked like a bride; none knew of the chain which I wore round my waist, a chain pulled tight enough to give me a touch of discomfort, to pinch occasionally, to remind me I am chained to Roger forever.

A collar might have been too obvious; we are nothing if not discreet. Roger has a reputation to uphold, after all. But we both knew about the chain; we both knew the symbolism, it added a thrill to the vows I took. Old fashioned vows, Clarisse, words which in your time were common, in my time are not. I vowed to obey.

My suit, in which we left for places far and wide, was dark green velvet, cut on the lines of riding suit from the late 1800s, matched with a hat adorned with a huge plume.

I had to advertise for a dressmaker to make the suit for me, no modern tailor would take it on; but an elderly lady who lives in a flat in Fleet Street (we are back to where it all happened!) answered the advertisement, and knew exactly what I wanted.

Society notes in the papers afterwards commented on the old fashioned yet beautiful appeal of the suit. It was, they said, right for the wife of a barrister, someone upholding the fine old traditions of our legal system. Roger thought so, too.

I wore it as a tribute to you, my enigmatic Clarisse.

We had a glorious honeymoon, or holiday if you like, cruising the sunshine places of the world, distant islands seeing exotic fruits flowers and people.

A strange honeymoon, some would say; for Roger did not come near me once. We shared a bed, and night after night he lay still and quiet, asleep I believe! while I lay next to him, buzzing and burning with desire, which he did not in any way appear to consider.

Two long weeks we sailed, Clarisse; imagine being next to your Cornelius for two whole weeks without his hands on your body! Oh, Roger kissed me, for sure he did, but he touched me nowhere else. And I dared not ask or mention it. I accept his word as my command, and if he chose not to touch me, then he would not do so.

When we got home, oh that was different! Then he became a Master, in every sense of the word.

Then he made up for lost time, then he called me to bed at every opportunity, until I was exhausted, and still he kept on. It thrills me to obey, Clarisse, as it did with you. It is a thrill whether it is for sex or for discipline.

It is a thrill to have Roger order me to decide on a punishment; my choice, his order. It thrills me to present Roger with a tawse, which I seem to prefer, despite the band of pain it creates when he thrashes me with it! As he does, hard, upwards of twenty strokes at a time. I crouch at his feet, offer up the instrument of discipline, allow him to decide whether it pleases him. If my choice does not please him then I get more than I would have had otherwise, so I work hard to please him! Imagine offering up a paddle, being turned down, and being caned twenty strokes instead!

Ah Clarisse, you never experienced the cane; always for you it was the riding crop, a slipper or the strap. A cane is thin, whippy, it cuts like nothing else, it is a line of fire springing across both cheeks at the same time. If I am very bad, Roger will cane my thighs, and that is pain beyond description. But why am I telling you? Nothing you will not have experienced, over and over again, and thrilled deep down inside even as I do when the Master speaks.

Some days he would order me out of bed early, fasten the chain around my waist, send me to work with orders which I had to obey. Judith was there to keep an eye on me, to ensure I did obey. Days I went without food, or drink, days I had to wear no shoes around the office, and endure everyone's comments; days I wore clothes which were too short for discretion and spent all the time trying to hide myself behind my desk.

Clarisse, one of the reasons I decided to write to you was to tell you how we are using your letters. I do not think in your wildest imagination you could have anticipated how your letters would be used.

We act out your scenes of discipline. That would please you, I think, and that is another reason I enjoy doing it.

One of Roger's friends lives in a converted church, not consecrated any more.

As often happens with Roger, he left the house for Chambers, leaving me a letter filled with orders. I had to attend this address (which I then didn't know) at precisely 5 pm, not a moment either way. Judith fortunately is very good about my orders; she lets me go without a word, despite raised eyebrows and comments from the other girls. But then a barrister's wife carries a lot of standing in a firm of Solicitors.

I took a taxi to the address, arrived far too early of course, and had to wait in the cold for half an hour. It was a cold day. Spring had arrived but not shaken off the coldness of winter.

I knocked on the door at 5 pm precisely.

The door was opened by a man I did not recognise, and I was ordered in.

The church had been cleared of furniture, and arranged with some pews, with a bench in the centre. Around it stood six men, Roger among them, but as always I looked down at the floor and did not acknowledge the existence of my Master.

Word for word they said the things in your letter, Clarisse, word for word they stung with their sharpness.

Finally I was laid across the bench, wrists and ankles tied at the corners, and my skirts turned back.

One at a time they gave me ten strokes each. I began to understand how you felt, but not entirely; for I am not new to the feel of the strap, and you were.

What was it like for you, Clarisse? What did you truly feel when the strap came down over and over again, burning and hurting as it did, on cheeks unused to the kiss of leather, the sting of birch? What I did appreciate was the total helpless feeling. Oddly, it was far worse than the time Roger summoned me to one of the 'trials' he staged regularly. This was colder, harder, this had no bystanders to applaud and smile, this was coldness, this was judicious thrashing of a wayward child. This was as close to what you experienced as a modern person could get.

And it hurt! The strap stung so much, as each used his full strength to lay into me, so helpless, so submissive to them all I hardly had voice with which to cry out. I now understand why you rejoiced in the memory of it, Clarisse, for the actuality of it was terrifyingly hard.

Afterwards, comforted by Roger, it was worth everything, when that thrusting member of his found my willing wetness, when the cheeks rose high off the bed to escape the pressure of the clothes and the pressure of his hips on mine, then I knew true ecstatic passion.

Remember your first initiation by Serenia?

Judith and I restaged that, using my flat above the office, Judith caressing and spanking, her white hand harder than it looks, then using her favourite paddle, leather covered, with holes dotted around the rim, holes which raise weals of their own.

We did your whipping in the stables too, one fine summer's day when the flies buzzed around the stable door, when straw and hay tickled my bare stomach as I pressed against the feeding troughs; smell of horse and leather, of dung and sheer manliness, as I held on tight to the wooden slats and the crop came down. That time Roger was harsh, my back and my legs took the strokes along with my usual well punished cheeks.

All this was leading up to another 'trial' at our home. Well, not so much a trial as a private party, with me as the centre piece of the show. This time Roger said it would be harsher than before, because I was more experienced.

I wonder how you would have coped with this one, Clarisse?

I was given a week in which I was not required to go to the office and work. During that week I had to wash and polish every inch of the house; walls, ceiling, furniture, carpets had to be shampooed or cleaned in some way. I had to prepare a dinner party meal for ten people, all friends of Roger's, all highly placed in the legal profession. Every night Roger checked the part of the house I had cleaned, looking for dust or missed dirt. I waited with bated breath for the inspection to be done, for fear of attracting further punishment if it was not right.

After all that, I had to ensure I was perfect, in a dress the exact copy of the one I wore last time, only in white. It took me an age to find it! but I did, in the end, I found it in a tiny shop in a corner of London you would have known as a village.

Roger didn't come near me again for the entire week, sometimes staying over in my flat rather than come home and be confronted with naked begging desire for his hands, his member, his whole beloved body on mine. But he knew me so well, knew how the frustration would build, knew it would add to the excitement of the day. Which it did, of course. Roger is not the supreme Master for nothing. I did contemplate using a candle, as you did once, but decided against it. I too wanted the excitement to build.

All this time I wore my chain, day after day, pinched tight around my waist. One day he telephoned and ordered me to put on nipple clamps and wear them until he said I could take them off. They were excruciatingly painful by the time he phoned again to say I could remove them. Nipple clamps, while washing the ceiling!

The day arrived: I cooked all day, prepared everything, chilled the wine, polished the glasses, set the table, before bathing and dressing myself. Silver jewellery, silver collar to replace the chain at my waist, silver nails, silver eye shadow, such cosmetics you may not have known, Clarisse, but which are effective if used properly. High heeled silver shoes completed the outfit.

No underwear at all.

The guests seemed very appreciative of the dinner I had cooked, those Lords and Ladies whose attention was partly on me, mostly on each other. I admired the ladies, so confident of themselves, laughing and joking, sending compliments in my direction as I served, poured, attended to their every need, all without saying a word. Roger said I must not speak, no matter what.

For his amusement and for the entertainment of the guests, I was punished between courses. Quite simply, I would bring in the soup or starter, serve everyone, then kneel down over the small padded footstool Roger liked to use. One or other guest would get up, walk over to me, bring a strap down five or six times and then go and sit down again, leaving me with burning stripes to sit at the table and consume my course.

As you can imagine, by the end of the dinner i was very red and very sore, as half of them had by then punished me, and hard too.

The ladies were at times harder than the men.

I cleared away, put everything in the dishwasher, a modern equivalent of Ruth, only not so friendly! and went back to the lounge where they all waited for me.

It is hard to describe my feelings. I was carrying on mundane jobs; clearing up, stacking the dishwasher, all the time knowing the ultimate test of endurance awaited me. I knew these guests would be severe, for they had already been hard on me, with stinging strokes of the strap to tell me they meant business. I wasn't allowed to beg for mercy, to ask them to stop, no matter what they did, and what they would do I did not know.

I was quivering with suppressed frustrated desire and sheer apprehension. A heady mixture, Clarisse! I guess you knew this well!

By this time my aching was intense, my need for relief from the frustration, the desire, overcoming all other feelings. The deep burning lust was something the pain had instilled in me. Submitting to these people, some of whom I have never met before, was in itself an experience to be savoured. To be punished while on show to others added a piquancy to the whole situation which was even more delightful. I was aware of wetness, and hoped no one would notice.

At Roger's command I took off my white dress and with it the cloak of innocence. Once again I rested over the footstool to await the pleasure of the guests.

One by one they came to me, all ten of them, each with different ideas and needs and desires which they enacted.

One spanked me, with a soft white hand which stung, especially over the severe strokes I had already received.

Another used the strap again, making me cry out in pain at each one.

Another used a leather soled shoe to spank my thighs until they were red and tingling.

Another used her gold chain to whip the insides of my thighs, more painful than any could believe.

Another used a hairbrush on my swollen sore cheeks, making me writhe in agony and cry out, but never for mercy, that was in itself forbidden.

It was the pleasure of one man to have me turn over, so he could use the strap on my breasts, which he did until they too glowed with heat and with lust.

Another used the tawse, a thicker version of your strap, Clarisse, which is my favourite and most feared instrument.

Another used the cane to cut, to wound, to hurt and to make me want to leap up - but it was not something I could do.

Another brought a martinet, fine strands of fine leather to whip my thighs on the front as well as on the back.

And lastly, the Judge whom I knew pulled out a small plaited whip and used that on my back.

Clarisse, I want you to know I laid there and took all this submissively; even though at times I longed to leave them all, to run and hide and weep and sob my pain into a pillow, but Roger's command held me there. I did protest, cry out, shouts which seemed to egg them on to greater and greater effort.

By the time they were done I was almost helpless with pain, and with crying. Every part of me hurt, my breasts have never been strapped in that way before. On Roger's orders I stood up, got dressed again, served drinks to my guests.

The feeling, oh Clarisse, the feeling! I came, I climaxed, upwards of six times, I am sure! while it went on. Some moments there were of pure pain, when I longed for release, other times the act of submitting to them, the combination of the deep burning and the helplessness of my position, made me feel the most wanted, the most loved, the most glowing of people in London that night!

Most important of all, more important than any of this, is the fact that that night Roger came to me. My orgasm was so intense that my body, apart from my shoulders and feet, left the bed in a huge arch of pure ecstasy.

I know now that my child was conceived that night.

I sit here in my own dressing room in Roger's home, at your table and on your chair, Clarisse, pondering the many roles we women play.

In your time you were wayward daughter, loving sister, companion, lover to both Serenia and Cornelius; you were the housekeeper, the supervisor when Ruth and others came to stay, you were Alfred's wife, and mother of Cornelius' child.

You were also Woman. Unlike many Victorian ladies, who stayed home and were no more than shadows of their husbands, you were Woman: determined, strong, full of life and love. Submit, you did that. Rejoice in it, you did that too.

I've done a lot of that. From secretary to Private Investigator, rejected lover through to friend and lover with Judith, to willing submissive to Roger, becoming a victim at one of his trials and an object of pleasure of his friends, I became Judith's friend and Roger's wife. At the same time I remained friends with people at the office, and daughter to my parents, for all that they are not here to see me now, gently curving with child. they will, they will be here when the date arrives for my child to thrust his way into the world.

He, or she? Another girl, another woman in the making, one I can initiate into the gentle art of submission and pure unadulterated giving? It will be hard to tell her how good it feels to give way to a man, for the modern women do not wish to think they are inferior to men.

In truth though, as you found, Clarisse, we are not inferior at all, but in our quiet and unobtrusive way the strongest of all. At any moment I could have turned my back on this life of submission, at any moment I could have said no, and it would have ended. I chose to be Judith's lover, Roger's lover, and slave to them both. It was my choice, not their dictate. Having made the decision to be a slave to them, I gave up responsibility for myself, again my own conscious decision.

I wish I could turn back the clock to that moment of that divorce, when the mother and daughter in law came out together, when they called the kind man I had seen all manner of ugly names. I would now say to her, go back, turn back the clock, try again. This time, don't stand up to your man and fight him, but give way, be submissive to him. His love will grow along with his power over you.

And perhaps the marriage would have survived, who knows? Or perhaps that man has found happiness with a wife who is submissive in her own way.

The truth is, we all show different faces to the world at different times. We all have many roles to play. They could have found a role to play together. But the will was not there; the love was not there, I think.

Enough. Too much speculation on things you would not understand.

Thank you, Clarisse, for your legacy to me. Thank you for being there, in spirit, in reality with these letters. Thank you for shedding light on your life, and helping me come to terms even more with mine.

My child kicks and turns within me, anxious to be free, to become a person in his own right. It is time I rested. I will close this now and will put it all away.

Who knows? One day I might get the letters out, put them together and put them in a book so other women will know your story and mine, perhaps experience the tapestry of pleasure and pain, pain and pleasure, so interwoven ...

You and I, Clarisse, the thread of our tapestry is woven into the warp of two centuries, is it not? But our desires for domination - are those warped desires, as many think? Ah no, I cannot believe that!

I drink to you, Clarisse, my brave Clarisse, and to the thrill that comes when the Master (or the Mistress) speaks!

The End